High School Daze

by

Robin Winberg

High School Daze
Author: Robin Winberg
Copyright © September 2008

Disclaimer

In no way does this novel advocate school violence. It is the writer's personal belief that there are two sides to every story, and both sides need to be told and understood in order for a complete picture to be perceived.

We may all be familiar with the devastation and chaos left in the wake of every school disaster. However, do we really truly understand what provoked these individuals into performing such heinous acts against their classmates? I, for one, am willing to try a variety of new techniques if it will help alleviate this tragic plight that has befallen us.

Manufactured in the United States of America

ISBN: 978-0-578-00175-3

Cover design by John Petersen

In Loving Memory of Louis John Ketchen

November 9, 1926 – October 1, 2008

Ja Che Koham, Dziadzi

To Shadow and Sera:

For showing me what really matters at the end of the day. I will always love and cherish you both for the wisdom you have bestowed on me and the unconditional love you have given me.

Chapter 1

"Open the doors! What's wrong with you?!" A panicked feminine

voice vociferated.

Rot in hell, bitch! Id fulminated.

My diaphragm emitted a low rumbling laughter as my eyes feasted on

the bodies falling to the floor...

Fry, bitches! *Fry*! Id squealed. We watched our peers as the gas took

over the oxygen. It was a wondrous sight to behold. The panic, the fear,

the realization that their lives were coming to an end. All I could do was

smile, and wonder if it occurred to them why the flicker of life was fading

from their eyes. Were they able to link the pain they felt with the pain I'd

been feeling all along? Or did they think I was just another one of those

students who killed everyone at their school because I was bad, or I had

snapped?

"Robin!" Mom's voice snapped at me, and I looked around for her as

my surroundings began to shake. "Robin!"

Slowly, the images of the school began to fade as the conscious realm came into focus. Their faces gave way to the four white walls that I had cried myself to sleep in.

It was a dream, I groggily thought to myself. My heart ached with the realization that the whole scenario was created from my subconscious as a coping mechanism.

"Are you okay?" Mom asked, concern resonating in her voice.

"Yeah." I whispered, closing my eyes.

"You were screaming in your sleep. You must have been having a nightmare."

Actually, it was a really good dream. Why the fuck did you wake her up? Id snapped.

"It wasn't that bad." I mumbled.

"Talk to me, honey. You were screaming 'fry' in your sleep. Was someone hurting you?" She asked, rubbing my shoulder.

"No, mom." Rolling over, I wanted to return to the beautiful images that my mind had entertained me with. "What time is it?"

"It's quarter after four. Try to get some sleep. We can talk about this in the morning." I felt her weight shift the mattress as the floor boards squeaked in accordance. "Good night."

"Night." I sighed. Even though I could still get 3 more hours of sleep, I knew it would be an exercise in futility. I wasn't going to be able to return, knowing that the happiest moment of my life had been nothing more than a dream.

My body was slow to comply with the demands of my brain. I ached for the strokes of my keyboard. While the spirit may have been willing, my flesh was very weak. Still, I was not about to give up this fight.

4

October 31, 2006 4:31am

Son of a bitch! I was having the best dream ever, and mom had to go and wake me up! I dreamed I killed everyone at school. It was awesome! In my dream, I hooked chlorine gas up to the vents at school, and everyone got sick. They were choking and throwing up and dying. I locked them inside the school, and I got to watch them die! I know, I shouldn't think that's a good thing, but those sons of bitches deserve it! All they do is hurt me, and I can't fucking take it anymore! Oh yeah. The trial went good, I guess. The bitch is spending time in jail. She's all upset. She has no right to be. She's the one that fucked up, not me. And now she has to pay the price. But Justin is her brother! I thought he was my friend, but it turns out he never cared about me! He was only using me to get inside info to help his sister! He flipped out on me in the middle of the courtroom! I'll show him! Next time in gym class, I'll show him. No more Miss Nice Girl. I'm going to show these sons of bitches the true meaning of pain!

Chapter 2

Unable to resume my nightly activities, I meandered downstairs to the kitchen. Spotting my morning sunlight in the dark brought a small measure of comfort as I poured a cup.

I don't like cold coffee, Id sneered.

So why don't you put it in the microwave? Superego offered. *That would warm it up.*

With my eyes closed, I navigated around the kitchen. I was too tired to function properly, and I was too stressed to sleep. I was caught in the world between the dead and the cognitive, lost without a map.

Through the cracks, I was able to locate the minute button. Pressing it twice, I heard the microwave jump into action. When the beep signified the time dictated had passed, I retrieved my warm nectar.

"It's barely 5am. What are you doing?" Mom asked, stumbling around. She was wearing her bathrobe, with a pair of slippers to match. Her hair resembled shag carpeting as it defied every ounce of control.

"Sorry. Can't sleep." I mumbled, sipping my coffee.

"Did the dream disturb you?" She asked, replaying my actions.

"No."

"Then why can't you sleep?"

I shrugged. I didn't know how to say that it broke my heart to know that it was just a dream, that the reality in the dream had brought me immeasurable comfort. Just to know that justice was served, regardless that it was imagined, was all I could ever ask for.

"What am I going to do with you?" Mom sighed, stirring her coffee.

"What?" I snapped. Her comment irritated me. How could she think I had done something wrong?!

"Honey, I know you had a bad dream. I woke you up. Talk to me. What's going on?" Her exasperation showed slightly.

"Mom. It wasn't a bad dream. It was a good dream." I grumbled.

"Then why were you screaming?" She pushed.

"Because a lot of stuff was happening." I took a sip.

"Are you sure?" She raised an eyebrow at me.

"Yes, I'm sure." I sighed.

"Okay, well how about you go get ready for school, and I'll make breakfast. What would you like to eat?" She offered a fake smile, trying to alleviate the seriousness of the situation.

"I'm not hungry." I turned in the direction of the upstairs bathroom, hoping to end this conversation and escape to the nice feel of hot water.

"Robin Rachael! You need to eat!" She snapped.

"And I said, I'm not hungry!" I snapped back.

"Come here! Sit down!" She pointed to a chair. Dragging my body in compliance, I rolled my eyes at her.

"What is going on?! You are being incredibly difficult! This isn't like you. I want answers NOW!" She folded her arms across her chest.

"What?" I folded mine, standing my ground.

"What's wrong? I know something is bothering you. Talk to me."

"Why should I make a big to do about getting ready for school when I have detention?" I snipped. "There's no point."

"Honey, I'm sure Mr. Mitchell felt he had a good reason to give you detention." Mom's voice softened.

"Why? Because I forgot that you gave me a cell phone? Oooo, what a reason!" Clenching my jaw, my vision became blurry as the rage inside of me gained power, threatening to take control.

"Well, they have a no cell phone rule…" Mom began.

"And I didn't fucking know that! I never used the damn thing! I never use the house phone! I don't have any friends! I never call anyone, and no one ever calls me! I didn't fucking do anything wrong! I was looking for a fucking pen so I could work on my English project! Excuse the hell out of me!" I screamed.

"Watch your language." Mom scolded. "So, you're saying you never used the cell phone I gave you?"

"No!" Whining, part of me wished I <u>had</u> gone back to sleep. This was brutal!

"Okay, and you weren't trying to make a call?" She asked.

"How could I? The phone died."

"And you're saying you forgot I gave you the phone, because you never use phones, so that's why you didn't call me instead of skipping classes?" She pressed.

"Yes." It took every ounce of strength I had not to bang my head against the table.

Sighing mom said, "Okay. Let me see if I can talk to Mr. Mitchell."

"Thank you. Can I go now?" I stood up.

"Yeah. Bye." She spat the words over her shoulder, slapping me in the face.

"What? What now?" I snapped.

"Nothing. I love you." She said from the cabinets.

"Yeah." I replied, running up the stairs. I had to find solitude, ASAP! I ran to the only place I knew I had privacy. My computer.

October 31, 2006 5:11am

I know I wrote less than an hour ago, but mom is pissing me off! She won't leave me alone! Geez! She keeps bugging me about not being happy to go to detention. Uh, duh! I wonder why! They gave me fucking detention for bullshit reasons! It doesn't matter how many times I say I was looking for a pen to do my homework. They don't care. They think I'm this evil child plotting to break all the rules. Yeah, keep it up. Keep saying I'm bad. See what happens! They don't fucking know me! Instead of judging me, maybe they should take the time to get to know me! They'll never do that. What do they care?

Chapter 3

Sitting in homeroom, all I could think about was detention. I wasn't looking forward to it. Sitting in the same room all day, asking for permission to get up to use the lavatory, not being able to talk or eat or do anything, was enough to break even the toughest kid.

While the attendant was making her rounds, I could see her dropping various colors of papers on different desks. Most of them were main office passes (blue). Mine, however, was orange.

Tilting my head to the right, I stared at the slip like a confused puppy. It read "Guidance Department" on it.

Strange. I wonder what they want. I thought. Then, the blue slip floated down to me. *I've been expecting you.* I glared at it.

Well, I shrugged to myself, *Since I got the orange slip first, I guess I'll go to the guidance department. Besides, I don't want to see Mr. Mitchell! Fucking asshole!*

Hearing the bell, I began my journey into a foreign part of the school. Across the hall from the cafeteria was the guidance department. I had seen the door before many times. However, I had never seen that door from the other side of it. *Well there's a first time for everything*, I thought.

Pushing through, there were several women hustling and bustling around the office. The emotional atmosphere was drastically different than that of the main office. It was as if they were antipodeans!

"Good morning." An older lady smiled at me.

"Hi." Returning her smile, I dropped the orange slip on her desk.

"Oh, goodie! A new-comer!" She beamed. Picking up the phone, she told another bright happy voice that I had arrived.

These people need to switch to decaf, Id sneered.

They're making the best of the situation, and I think they're doing a commendable job. Superego scolded.

"Robin?" A younger woman poked her head out from around the hallway inside the guidance office. She had long blond hair that cascaded down her back, and bright blue eyes. While she was only a few inches taller than me, the few years she had on me made her a bit intimidating. The lady had on black dress slacks with a bright peach sweater. Turning to face her, she said, "Right this way." Following her disappearing act led us to a modern office. It had weird art on the walls, and there was a radio

playing "bubble gum pop music" somewhere in the room.

"Have a seat." She said, flopping in her oversized chair. "Hi, my name

is Miss Benton. You can call me Jeannette." She thrusted her hand out in

an over enthusiastic greeting. An unseen impetus compelled me to give

her mine. Her hand was chilly and frail, but she shook mine firmly.

"So, what seems to be going on?" Jeannette voice had a lilt at the end

of every sentence. She retrieved a note pad and a pen from inside her desk.

She keeps going on at this rate, I'm going to be sick. Id whined.

Shut up. Superego retorted.

I shrugged. I had no idea what she was asking, or why I was even here.

"Well, your mother called the guidance office this morning and said

you've been unusually difficult and belligerent. Is that true?" She asked,

slightly pouting.

"Not really." I shook my head.

"Okay. She must have been concerned for a reason. Why do you think

that is?" She asked, positioning her pen.

"I don't know." I shrugged again.

"Hm, okay. Well, tell me what's been happening in school lately." She scribbled something on the pad of paper.

"Nothing, really." I looked around the office, not making an effort to conceal my boredom.

"Okay, well then tell me what grade you're in." She smiled.

"Ninth."

"This is your first year! How exciting!" She beamed.

"Okay." I maintained the same generic inflection in my voice. It was as if Mr. Mitchell was speaking through me.

"How do you feel about being in the ninth grade?"

"I don't really care." I shrugged.

"You're not excited? How come?" She pouted.

I remained silent, unsure of what to say.

Oh, geez. I wonder. This place sucks. The people sucks. You suck! Id griped, rolling her eyes.

"Well, what do you and your friends like to do outside of school?" She asked, tilting her head to the left. Her hair swung across her shoulder in accordance with her movements.

"I don't have any friends." I looked down at the floor, the truth stinging my heart like a scythe.

"Not one?" She asked incredulously. I don't think she took me seriously.

I shook my head.

"Well, then. What can we do to help you make friends?" She smiled. She was really perky. It was starting to annoy me. I mean, honestly, who is that cheerful first thing in the morning?!

I shrugged.

"How about an after school activity?"

I shook my head again.

"Okay, is there anyone in any of your classes you'd like to become friends with?"

A mental scan of all of the peers I knew made me want to jump over her desk and strangle her. *If she knew the hyenas I attended class with, she wouldn't dare to ask me such a dumb question.* I thought. My head kept moving side to side, indicating the same answer over and over.

"Hmm... well, what do you like to do?" She asked.

"Nothing."

"What do you do for fun when you're not at school?"

"Play solitaire." I shrugged.

"What else?" She tilted her head to the left, batting her styled eyelashes innocently.

"Nothing."

"Hm, okay…" She scribbled something else on the pad, and then paused to ponder for a moment. I continued to look around the room, distracting myself from the annoyance and anger building up inside of me. Who was she? What did she care about what I was experiencing in this hell? Furthermore, what could she do to alleviate my burdens?

"Well, do you have any acquaintances? You know, people you talk to in school, but not outside of school?" She asked with a smile.

It was as if she drove the pen in her hand through my ribcage. My thoughts flooded to Justin, and the events that had transpired at the courtroom. Tears began to well in my lower eyelids and I dropped my head, hoping my hair would conceal the pain.

She must've noticed it, because the happiness fled her face as she became eerily silent. The silence continued to grow as time marched forward.

"Well, how about we call it a day?" Her voice was barely above a whisper, having lost her obnoxious enthusiasm. Looking up at her, she pulled the corners of her mouth upwards slightly.

I nodded. For the first time, we were in agreement.

Standing up, she walked me back to the main part of the guidance department. The receptionist was still beaming, despite the distress written broadly all over my face.

"Where are you headed, dear?" She smiled.

"The main office." I handed her the blue hall pass I had received in homeroom.

"Okay." She wrote down the time and signed it, returning it to the hand of mine that was waiting nearby.

"Enjoy your day!" She smiled as I walked out the door.

Yeah, because every day is a wonderful day here. I thought bitterly.

Numbly, I trudged down the hall. My brain had too many questions regarding the visit to the guidance office. Unfortunately, I had no answers. Why was I called down there? Jeannette had answered that one. Mom had called the school, saying she was concerned about me. But why did Jeannette think I would talk to her? Because I won't talk to mom? What did Jeannette hope to accomplish by talking to me? Would she try to talk to me again in the future? If I did talk to her, would it make a difference?

Walking into the main office, I spotted a familiar face. I offered a temporarily smile to the receptionist as I gave her the hall pass the guidance department had recently signed.

"We were wondering where you were." She smiled back at me. "I'll let Mr. Mitchell know you're here." Taking my seat, I knew it wouldn't be long before my newest best friend graced me with his presence.

"Ms. Edwards?" Mr. Mitchell's familiar face showed itself from behind his office door. I followed him into my destiny, where trouble waited impatiently for me.

"Sorry I was late. I got a slip to go see the Guidance Department." I said upon entry.

"Next time, report here first." Mr. Mitchell's monotone echoed slightly in the lifeless office.

"I'm sorry. I didn't know." I apologized again.

"It's okay." Shifting in his chair, he picked up a piece of paper. "According to attendance, you weren't here on Tuesday."

I stared blankly at him. I already knew I didn't attend detention, and I knew I was going to get more detention for skipping detention.

"Where were you?" He asked.

"I was at home. I had to testify on Wednesday, and I wanted to prepare for it." I lied.

"That's odd. Your mother didn't mention it when I spoke to her earlier." He frowned. My heart froze with panic. Was I already caught in my lie?

"What'd mom say?" I asked nonchalantly, trying to conceal the panic. I tried to gauge the damage, seeing if there was any way I could get away with it.

"She believes it wasn't fair of you to receive detention for the cell phone incident. Your mother said according to the bill, you haven't made one phone call. Not to her, not to anyone, and that when you took it out of your purse, it was most likely by accident." He kept staring at the paper. I wasn't sure what was on it that was so fascinating.

The left corner of my mouth pulled up slightly. It was nice to see that Mom was trying to spare me detention. It was nice to see that she had my 'back'. This time.

"So I'm going to assign you one day of In School Suspension for skipping the day you missed. If you bring in a note from your mother, then I will dismiss it." Mr. Mitchell put down the paper. "Just don't be missing any more classes, okay?"

"Yes, sir." I smiled big at him, hoping it would make me seem agreeable. *Now I have to get mom to write me a note. This ought to be fun.* I thought.

"You'd better get going to your class before you're too late." He stood up.

"I'm hurrying!" I smiled, zipping out the door. Rushing up to the receptionist, she was already one step ahead of me.

"Take care." She smiled at me as I grabbed the hall pass from her hand.

Not that I cared. I was in a hurry to get to study hall. I had two study halls every day, and I never had much homework to do. At least, not enough to warrant needing that much time.

When I finally made it to the cafeteria entrance, the bell rang. *Damn it!* I grumbled. *"They're going to think I skipped first period, and I'm going to have to go see Mr. Mitchell tomorrow! Damn, damn, damn!"*

Sighing, I tossed the hall pass on the attendant's desk and flopped down in my own. Taking out a sheet of paper, I turned to my only friend; my thoughts.

October 31, 2006 8:45am

Geez, this is turning into a craptacular morning! First, mom wakes me up from an awesome dream! Then she won't get out of my face about why school pisses me off! Then she calls the Guidance Department because I'm pissed off! Uh, duh! If you had to deal with this shit, you'd be pissy, too! On the bright side, I won't have detention if I can get mom to write me a note. Hopefully, she will. If she agrees with me that I shouldn't have had detention at all, then maybe she won't be so mad about me skipping. We'll have to see.

Chapter 4

I paced the living room floors, waiting to hear the garage door. All day, I ached to know why I had been called down to the guidance department. The only information they had offered was that mom had sicken them on me. I wanted to know why.

A few minutes after her normal arrival time, I heard the electronic shifting of the garage gears. My head spun around to the kitchen, where I knew the door would open to reveal Mom.

"Hey!" I yelled, running across the first floor of the house.

"Hey yourself. How was school?" She asked, closing the door.

"It was okay. Why did the guidance department call me down?" I blurted out, furrowing my eyebrows.

"I just thought maybe you would talk to them about what was going on. You won't talk to me." She shrugged.

I would if you'd listen. I thought angrily.

"Talk about what?" I asked.

"I don't know. Whatever's bothering you." She shrugged again.

I sighed. It wasn't that I objected to discussing what was 'bothering' me. In fact, I ached to talk about what was going on. The only catch that prevented me was when anyone gave me a retort. If they wanted to know what was going on, they wouldn't try to justify the opposing side. I didn't want to play "point, counterpoint." There were no opposing views when it came to ones' feelings. And the fact that they always had something to say about what I was saying made me feel like what I was saying wasn't that important. So if it's not that important, why bother saying it at all?

"Well, I don't want to talk to them." I said, turning my attentions to the cabinets. It was too early to go to sleep, and I couldn't walk off in the middle of a conversation to escape to my computer. The only friend I had left was food.

"Why not?" Mom asked.

"I don't know them!" I exclaimed, smiling. I don't know why I smiled. It escaped with the words.

"So get to know them, goober!" She smiled back at me.

"I just want to be left alone." My eyes opened wide like a puppy's, pleading with her.

"So, what's on the agenda for tonight?" She ignored my pleas.

I rolled my eyes at her. "What's for dinner?"

"You're always hungry!" Mom laughed at me. "What do you want for dinner?"

"I don't know. That's why I'm asking." I laughed.

"How about pizza?"

"Sounds good." I parted my lips in a big smile.

"Okay. Go get ready. I'll meet you in the car." Mom headed out the garage, and I ran upstairs to fetch my shoes.

Upon entry of my safe haven, the glow of the monitor called to me. It begged to create a rapport, and I couldn't resist complying.

October 31, 2006 5:51pm

Mom says she called the guidance department because she thinks I want

someone to talk to. I told her I want to be left alone, but she ignored me.

I'm serious! I don't want to talk to anyone! They don't care! They always

tell me, 'Oh, well blah blah blah.' Like I almost care about that crap! I

don't. If you want to know how I feel, then don't try to tell me anything

else. You're asking for information. I'm not asking about how the other

kids feel! If they're being assholes and hurting me, then why would I care

about how they feel? I'm not hurting them. I could. Hehehe....

Chapter 5

As the car slowly rolled along the streets, I clutched my book bag. I knew I had neglected to relay the message Mr. Mitchell gave me, and time was running out. My fingertips couldn't focus on one piece of fabric. They had to run amuck.

"Hey mom?" I asked, trying to break the nervous ice.

"Yes, dear?" Her eyes remained focused on the road.

"Can I have a note?" I lightly bit the inside of my lip.

"For what?" She snipped, her exasperation apparent.

"Tuesday."

"What about Tuesday?" She slowed to comply with a red light.

"I was supposed to have detention, but Mr. Mitchell said that you called him and said it wasn't fair for him to give me detention for the cell phone since I never used it." I didn't know how to articulate the entire picture without upsetting her, so I only gave her pieces for the time being. And the pieces weren't in chronological order.

"So you want me to write you a note?" She asked, sighing.

"Yes please." I replied.

"If you weren't in detention, where were you?" She asked.

Damn! I'm going to have to tell her I stayed home after she kept insisting I get ready to go to school! She's going to know I lied to her, and she's going to get pissed! Damn! Damn! I thought.

"Home." I bit my lip a little harder in anticipation of her ire.

"So you skipped school?" Was that annoyance I heard?

"Sorry. I was so nervous about the trial that I wanted to stay home and prepare!! I know you and Cindy told me not to worry and relax, but I couldn't help it!" I shrugged, smiling. "I wanted to get everything perfect!"

That's right. Play to the accountant side, the side that has to have everything perfect. Maybe she'll admire that quality, since she exhibits it herself. Smart thinking. Id nodded.

That's horrible. You're purposefully deceiving her for your own gain. Superego shook her head.

Welcome to the real world. Everybody does that. That's how they communicate. Nobody says what they mean, or mean what they say. They propose sentences based on what they want, but they've already predetermined how the other person is going to react. It sucks, but that's how people talk to each other. I shrugged at their views of the truth.

"Why were you worrying?" Mom asked.

"I told you, mom! Every time somebody does something to me and they get in trouble, somebody else is going to react! They don't like their friends getting in trouble! And yeah, they're the ones who are wrong, but that's not going to stop them!"

"I know. That's why we went to trial. To try and tell everyone that's it's not acceptable to behave that way." Mom smiled.

"Can I have the note?" I asked again, not sure if she's forgotten that I'd asked.

"This time. Next time you're worried about something, I want you to talk to me, okay?" She sighed.

"Yes, mom." I smiled. Digging around in my bag, I pulled out a loose leaf sheet of paper. I wanted to secure that note!

When we reached the school, I handed her the paper. She wrote the necessary information, then handed it back to me.

"Thanks, mom." I pushed open the door, eager to rub Mr. Mitchell's face in my newly acquired "get out of detention free card."

"Hey." Mom said.

"Yeah?" I stopped, turning around to look at her.

"Give me a hug." She outstretched her arms. Leaning in, she kissed the top of my head. "I love you."

"Love you too, mom." With a smile and a wave, I ran to homeroom. I knew there were more pieces of paper I could scribble down on.

November 1, 2006 7:36am

Haha! I can't wait to give Mr. Mitchell the note mom gave me! Fucking

asshole thinks I'm going to rot in detention for every little reason his pea

brain can come up with! I don't think so! Not this time, jackass! You can

go rot in hell for all I care! You don't fucking know me! So stop trying to

send me to detention! I'm not doing anything wrong! And I have the note

to prove it! I'll play your game. Except I'll win. Hahahahahaha…..

Chapter 6

Like a peacock, I sat in homeroom. I knew I would be receiving a blue slip for missing first period yesterday, and I knew that I wouldn't be receiving detention. Not this time. I had been in the guidance department the day before. And I also had my note ready from my mother. I wouldn't be going to In School Suspension. I was free and clear!

It glided through the air and landed on my desk. This was the first time that I wasn't afraid of it. I wasn't upset or nervous. I knew I had that blue pass beat.

Hey Mr. Mitchell. Screw you. I smiled at the pass.

It remained placid on the desk.

Hearing the bell, I gathered the pass in my left hand right in front of the note. The note overshadowed the pass, coming out victorious in sheer size.

With my head held high, I marched to Mr. Mitchell's office. I couldn't control my arrogance. I anticipated the outcome to be in my favor for the very first time.

"Good morning." I smiled at the receptionist.

"Oh, Ms. Edwards! What are you doing here?" She smiled back at me.

"Mr. Mitchell asked for this note yesterday." I said, dropping moms' excuse in her hands. "And I'm guessing this pass is for missing first period yesterday. But I was in the guidance department! Then I came here!" I smiled.

"Okay. I'll give Mr. Mitchell the note. And I do remember you being here yesterday, so I'll cross your name off the list." She winked at me.

"Thank you." I winked back.

"You'd better get going to class before you're late." Other students who had received blue passes were starting to arrive.

"Can I have a pass? Just in case. I don't want to get marked as late, and then show up tomorrow!" I offered a small fake laugh.

"Sure." She wrote the time on my pass and signed it. "Just so you know though, tomorrow's Saturday. Nobody has school tomorrow."

My gut seized, an unseen force upper cutting my diaphragm. I had completely lost track of time! I had been so preoccupied with the trial and with avoiding detention that I had forgotten to complete my English project! If I had any hope of passing it (with or without Andrew), I was going to need my solitude in study hall!

"Thank you!" Taking the note, I rushed out the door. I was too focused on <u>not</u> failing the project that I couldn't take delight in it being Friday.

As I ran through the halls, I mentally reviewed the progress I had made. What else did I need to accomplish in order to get a decent grade? I knew it wasn't feasible for me to illustrate the story line, not in the short amount of time I had left. But I was determined to get the best grade I could with the final countdown.

I dropped the hall pass on the attendant's desk. Without saying a word, I flopped down in my seat. My heart was heavy with doubt as I rummaged for paper. My subconscious knocked at the door in the forefront of my mind, trying to remind me of the exact moment that I became obsessed with my grades.

We walked down the corridor, admiring the collages my class had decorated the walls with. My second grade teacher had the entire class do a project on an animal of their choice and had displayed them for all the parents to see.

Mom beamed as she tiptoed project to project, admiring the work of all the children. Dad wasn't interested. He was only concerned with my project.

"Which one did you do?" Dad's voice was gruff and low, the seriousness of his attitude painfully obvious. I pointed down the hall, spotting the koala picture I had pasted on the cover.

Walking away from us, he stood in front of it. As he looked it over, he remained silent and still. It was always impossible to judge his reaction.

"You got an A." He said. His eyes always contained the same emotional response, or lack there of. They were solid brown with short eyelashes, but they were hardened by the bitter disappointment life had offered them over the years. Everyone who looked into them experienced the same cold shiver run down their spine.

"Oh, honey! Congratulations!" Mom exclaimed with a smile, her whole face lighting up.

"Why wasn't it an A+?" The same lack of expression that was in his statement filled his question.

"Oh, Dan! She got an A! Can't you be happy about that?" Mom put her hands on her hips. "Besides, her teacher doesn't do plusses or minuses. Just letter grades. Our little girl did perfectly." Smiling at me, she tousled my hair.

It was too late. My heart sank. It was every child's dream to get good grades, to make their parents proud. That was all I could have hoped for.

It seemed insignificant now. I had put so much effort in the project. All the happiness and pride I had felt on the car ride over had been dashed across the walls, cozying up to the other projects. They seemed so much better than mine now.

Next time, I'll do better. I'll get that A+. I swore to myself.

Ever since then, I was in a constant state of unrest. Every time a teacher mentioned the word "project", I was on high alert. Every time, I received an A. I would curse silently to myself, and imagine a + next to the grade to pacify Id. I always promised that next time, I would see that sign. Next time…

In a fever, my hand flew across the pages. My brain barked orders almost faster than my hand could comply, but the team worked at the speed of light to ease me of my fear of failure.

When their work had been completed, I glanced up at the clock. I had ten minutes to examine their progress and see if it met my standards. With a few nods and a couple omissions, their work was acceptable. Now I had to rewrite it in legible handwriting. With painstaking effort, I rewrote the entire story. I made sure every word had enough space from the word in front and behind it.

I wonder if Andrew will get any credit. He didn't do any of the work. I pondered to myself.

Fuck him. Id shrugged.

Hey now! That's not nice! Superego scolded.

The bell rang, shooing me off to my second period class.

Don't worry, dear. You have another study hall to finish the project. Maybe you can even include some of your own artwork. Superego smiled.

Haha! That's funny! She doesn't have study hall, dumbass! Id grinned. *Better get moving to gym.*

My feet were glued to the floor by the sudden electric current that ran through my body. As my body began to tingle, my stomach seized. I couldn't breathe or move.

With every ounce of strength I could muster, I blocked the phobia from my mind and slowly moved towards the gym. I forced my mind to go clear, erasing all thoughts about Justin and the trial. I shoved the "What if?" monster back into the far corners of my mind. My heart protested as the gym doors came in visual range. My appendages revolted, thrashing against the commands my brain had given them.

Walking in the gym, I looked around. I saw several familiar faces, but I didn't see his.

It'll be okay. You don't have to talk to him. Superego tried to comfort me.

You could punch him in his face. Id offered her own comfort.

Violence never solved anything. Don't you get that by now? Superego snipped.

You don't have to use physical force to leave a scar. Don't you get that by now? Id retorted. *What's worse? Having a scar on the outside of the body where everyone can see it and know that it's healed, or having a scar on the inside where no one can see it, so no one knows if it's healed or not?*

I understand what you're trying to say. Using words as weapons can leave scars on a person's soul. However, just because they hurt you, it doesn't justify you hurting them. Superego had a retort of her own.

And there comes a point when a person can't take anymore emotional scarring. So they lash out. Just like an abused animal in a corner. The soul doesn't want to be restrained in the corner by pain, so it will lash out to escape. And if these assholes keep it up, what do you think my girl here is going to do to get away from the pain? Id put her hands on her hips.

There's no reasoning with you. Superego sighed.

Trying to hide against the wall, I impatiently waited on my side of the gym for class to begin.

"Hey, bitch." Justin sneered. His beautiful green eyes hissed with anger.

I just stared at him, not saying anything.

"I just thought you'd like to know that my sister got jumped in prison because you're a little snitch and can't take a fucking joke." His taunts continued.

I remained silent.

"You'd better watch your ass. Nobody in here is happy that my sister is in jail. And it's all because of you." Laughing, he walked away.

Dropping my head to the floor, I allowed my hair to fall in my face. Hopefully, it hid the tears welling up in my eyes. That is, until I could suppress the pain and the rage inside.

The whistle screaming at us jerked my head up, and a lone tear jumped from my right eye. "Alright kids. Today, we're playing baseball. Line up against the wall so that we can divide everyone into two teams." The teacher shouted.

Everyone leaned against the wall, and the teacher chose two students. "Okay. Mike and Abby are team captains. They'll take turns choosing their teams until everyone is divvied up. Abby, would you like to choose your first teammate?" She smiled.

I watched Mike and Abby choose everyone else around me until I was the last one standing against the wall, unchosen. Although it was Abby's turn, she didn't call my name. She just stared at me, unblinking. I sadly stared back into her hollow uncaring eyes.

"Go ahead, Robin. You're on Abby's team." The teacher chirped. "Good luck, teams!"

That's so sad. I don't know why nobody chose you. You are a really good person. Superego shook her head.

Gee, I wonder. Because they suck and no one gives a shit. Id rolled her eyes.

Throughout the rest of gym, I was a soulless zombie. Physically, I was present, my body complying with the movement demands imposed by my "team" and by the teacher. My soul had curled up in the bottom of my torso in the fetal position and began to cry. Nothing I could do would alleviate my soul from the hellish torture it was going through. Nothing anyone could do could alleviate it.

"Good game. See you next class." The teacher dismissed us. As I walked back to the bleachers to retrieve my book bag, I heard a voice call out, "See you next class, Robin!"

Turning to the direction of its origin, I saw Justin waving. A couple of his friends were laughing. Once again, my eyes took in the sights south of themselves as I trudged off to English.

Not if I kill you first. Id hissed, her anger rising up in me. *I told you not to trust him.*

Stop that! You can't threaten to kill other students! What do you think people would do to you if they knew that's what you were thinking? They'd lock you up! They'd take you seriously and put you away so you couldn't hurt anyone! Superego whispered loudly.

I wasn't talking out loud. You two are the only people who can hear me. Nobody knows that I want to hurt him. Besides, why do you think I haven't said anything? I'm not stupid. I know they'll lock her away somewhere. Especially after what the other kids did at their schools. Id snorted.

I'm just saying. Try to find an alternative solution. Superego whispered.

I'm just saying, shut the fuck up. Id rolled her eyes.

Nervously, I entered English. I desperately wanted an A+, but my subconscious told me that it wasn't possible. The point of this assignment was to work as a team, but Andrew was only about himself.

Slowly, I retrieved the project out of my book bag. My soul was still crying from last period, and I knew that this class wasn't going to make its pain load any lighter.

"Good morning." Mrs. Grant smiled. "Is everyone excited that it's Friday?"

Some students mumbled positive messages, indicating some level of enthusiasm.

"Good." She beamed. "I hope everyone is ready to present their projects to the class."

Hearing those words, my soul stopped crying. I had to get up and present to the entire class?! Could this day get any worse?

"Who would like to go first?" Looking around, she called on another pair of students. I breathed a quiet sigh of relief for the temporary reprieve.

As they discussed their skateboarding snake, Mrs. Grant snuck up on me.

"Were you and Andrew able to complete your project?" She whispered in my ear.

"I did." I pushed the papers in her direction.

"This was supposed to be a group project." She whispered.

I looked at her, batting my eyelashes in innocence. I was at a loss for words, unable to explain why Andrew didn't participate.

"Well, how does this sound? For your efforts, I'll give you a C+. Because Andrew didn't contribute, I'll give him an F. At least you passed." She smiled at me. Standing, she made her way over to Andrew's desk. He didn't look pleased after they were finished with their conversation.

My soul began bawling in its epidermal shell. A C+?! That was an atrocious grade! I had worked so hard on it!

"Wonderful!" Mrs. Grant started to clap, signaling the rest of the students to applaud. "Next we'll hear from Robin."

Standing, I gathered my papers and sulked to the front of the room. Andrew didn't move from his desk.

Great. So everyone's going to be staring at me. I thought.

Stuttering, I managed to trip over my words long enough to get through the entire presentation. I kept wondering if Andrew blamed me for the F he received, but I had no way of knowing.

"Absolutely delightful!" Mrs. Grant clapped.

The bell rang, saving the rest of the students from the embarrassment I went through.

"We'll hear more of them on Monday. Have a good weekend." Mrs. Grant smiled.

My heart broke as I walked back to my desk. The tears that were threatening to flood from my eyes in gym class had returned, except this time, I couldn't force them back.

Fumbling around in my purse, I reached for my cell phone and dialed mom's work #. I wanted to go home. Since the adults wanted me to call my mother in times of an emergency, I decided to give their way a shot.

"Hello?" Her sweet voice was a reprieve from the obviousness of my breaking heart.

"Hi, mom." I barely spoke above a whisper.

"What's wrong honey?" She asked. Concern flooded her voice.

"I want to go home!" My voice cracked, and tears ran freely down my cheeks.

"I'm getting ready for an audit. Is it important?" She asked, sighing impatiently.

"I want to go home!" I repeated, sobbing.

"Okay, okay. Meet me in the lobby. I'll be there as soon as I can."

Hanging up the phone, I ran to my locker to dispose of any reminders. I wasn't about to take my book bag home and listen to the ghosts of previous school days as they repeatedly tortured my broken soul.

Pacing the lobby floors for what seemed to be an hour, Mom finally arrived. I ran into her arms, seeking solace.

"Honey, what happened?!" She asked, wrapping her arms around me.

"I want to go home." The only words I could speak, I uttered. My tears flowed again with a renewed force.

"Alright. Go wait in the car. I'll go tell the main office that I'm taking you home." As she headed in the direction of Mr. Mitchell, I ran out the front doors. When I reached the car, I jumped inside. I was grateful for the four metallic walls that offered some emotional protection. Burying my head in my arms, I began to sob loudly until Mom entered the driver's side.

"Would you mind telling me what happened?" Mom asked, climbing in.

"A lot of stupid crap." I sniffled.

"Like what? You're really upset!" Mom petted my hair.

I just shook my head. I didn't know how to articulate everything that had happened today. I didn't understand myself. I was so happy to have finally beaten Mr. Mitchell as his game of constantly handing out detention, but 2 hours later, I couldn't stop crying. Had what happened been that bad?

The rest of the car ride was ridden in silence. The only sounds to be heard were the revving of the engine and mom's fingers gliding past my ears.

A calming tranquility rushed over me as we pulled in our driveway.

"Call me at lunchtime, okay?" Mom asked.

"I will. Thank you mom." I leaned in, giving her a hug.

"Tonight, we'll talk. I want to know what happened, okay?" She looked straight into my eyes, petting my cheek.

"Okay." I looked down at her seatbelt buckle.

"I love you. Hope you feel better." She smiled.

"Love you too." I dashed to my computer as fast as I could carry my weight. I didn't stick around long enough to hear mom leave.

November 1, 2006   10:13am

Today was awful! It started out good. That should've been my first clue that it wasn't going to be a good day. I was able to get out of having detention. I'm sure that pissed Mr. Mitchell off. But I got a C+ on my English project because Andrew didn't help me, and it's supposed to be a "team thing". That's bullshit! I get a bad grade because he's a useless fuck! And I saw Justin today. He said his sister got beat up in jail, and that it's my fault. He said he was going to get some people to beat me up so I knew how his sister felt! Um, I know how his sister feels. She slammed my eye into my locker! I can't go back to that school! What am I going to do?

Chapter 7

After I had emotionally vomited all over my computer, I was exhausted. I decided to lie down in bed and try to relax.

I must have fallen asleep, because the next thing I knew, Mom was sitting on my bed.

"Morning, sunshine." She smiled at me.

"Hi." I reached upwards, elongating my skeletal frame like a cat.

"You didn't call me at lunch." Mom frowned.

"Sorry. I must've fallen asleep." I rolled over to face her.

"I figured. So, do you mind telling me what happened earlier?"

For a split second, my mind drew a blank, and then everything came flooding back to me. My face wrinkled in emotional agony as the memories fought to replay themselves first.

"You mentioned something about a C+?" Mom pressed for more details.

"Yeah. Remember how I told you I had to do a project in English class?" My mind slowly began processing the events that had transpired earlier that day.

"I remember. You said you were looking for a pen in detention when you accidentally took your phone out." Mom nodded.

"Well, I guess because my partner didn't work with me, I got a bad grade. It was supposed to be about teamwork, but he didn't work with me. So I got a bad grade!" I pulled the blankets up angrily, clutching them tightly against my locked jaw.

"Oh, honey. A C+ isn't that bad. It's still passing." Mom smiled sympathetically at me.

"Why punish me? It's not my fault he's a dumbass and didn't do any work!" I pouted.

"Watch your language. You're too pretty to be using ugly words like that, and you're smart enough to think of other words to use to express yourself." She scolded, sounding like a broken record. "That can't be the only thing that upset you. Did something else happen?"

I imagined Justin's sneering face floating in front of me, and the tears returned.

"Oh, honey. Don't cry." Mom leaned in to hug me. "Talk to me."

"I spent all of first period study hall on my project. I didn't talk to anyone. I didn't bug anyone. I didn't say a word. I sat there and did my work. And I went to second period gym. I was standing against the wall. I wasn't talking to anyone. I wasn't bugging anyone! And he came up to me out of nowhere!" I started to sob.

"Who did?" Mom began petting me, trying to soothe my cries.

"Justin! He said that his sister got jumped, and I'd better watch it because someone will do it to me!" My sobbing grew louder as my words tumbled out, forcing both of them to compete over attention and clarity.

"Somebody else is threatening you?!" Mom asked incredulously. Pulling away from me, she leaned back far enough to visually absorb the pain radiating from my soul. Standing up, she began to pace. "I can't believe this! This is ridiculous! I wonder if the parents know how deplorably their children are behaving!"

"I don't want to go back there, Mom. Can't I transfer to a different school or something?" I sniffed, wiping my eyes on my sleeve. My lungs shuttered as I struggled to inhale.

"Why would you want to do that?" She spun around on her heels and looked at me, confused.

"I don't want to get 'jumped.' I'm tired of being picked on. I just want to be left alone." I looked up at her, my lower lip quivering in sadness.

"Honey, you can't run away from your problems. They will follow you wherever you go. We need to fix this. Then, if you want to transfer at the end of this year, we can talk about it over the summer." Mom sat back down on the bed.

"We can't fix this. Nothing we can do will make them stop and leave me alone." Walking over to my computer desk, I grabbed a tissue and blew my nose.

"Honey, we <u>will</u> fix this. I promise you. One way or another, we will fix this." Mom smiled at me.

That's right. One way or another, we'll fix this. Id smiled back at her.

"What's for dinner?" I sniffled, the corner of my mouth pulling slightly upward.

"You're always hungry!" Mom laughed at me, throwing at pillow. My reaction time wasn't quick enough as it bounced off of my button nose.

"That doesn't answer the question." I threw the pillow back.

"What do you want?" Mom asked.

"Mashed potatoes and chicken gravy!" I laughed.

Mom just rolled her eyes at me.

"Please?" I pushed my bottom lip out and batted my eyelashes, chasing her as she made her way downstairs to the kitchen.

"Fine. You know you need to expand your eating horizons to more than just the same few things." She shook her head at me.

"I will. Someday." I grinned at her.

"Can you peel me some potatoes?" She asked.

"Sure." As I reached in the cabinet for the potatoes, I couldn't shake the worry that lingered in the back of my mind. What was mom going to do about Justin? Would she be able to stop the other students' assaults? Was an end to this madness in sight?

"Hey mom?" I asked, taking a knife out of the silverware drawer.

"Yes dear." She smiled at me.

"What's going to happen now?" With simple strokes, the skin of the potatoes flew into the garbage can.

"What's going to happen with what?" She asked, furrowing her brows.

"What I told you Justin did." Superego thought it would be easier if I danced around the subject, rather than to face the sting of his betrayal again.

"Well, I'm going to have to talk with Mr. Petersen about it. And we're going to have to come up with a better solution than having the police patrol the hallways. Obviously, they aren't protecting the students as well as they think they are if these things keep happening." She shook her head in disgust.

"I was just wondering." I shrugged.

"What do you want to happen?" She asked.

"I don't know. Like I said, I just want things to stop. I just want to be left alone."

"I'm glad we talked, honey. You know you can come and talk to me anytime." She smiled at me.

"Yeah." I kept peeling the potatoes.

November 1, 2006 7:49pm

So I told mom what happened at school today. She said she's going to talk to Mr. Petersen again. I doubt that'll do any good. It didn't do a damn thing the first time she talked to him. What's the difference now? Anyways, I hope she figures something out. It would be nice to just get through high school unscathed. I'm not trying to pick fights with the other students. I go to school, I take notes in class, I don't talk to anyone, and I leave everyone alone. Why can't they leave me alone? I don't know what I'm going to do if they don't. I can't take much more of this. What if mom talks to Mr. Petersen, and someone beats me up for it? What if Justin gets in trouble, and someone else retaliates? This is a never ending cycle. I'm never going to get out of it!

Chapter 8

"Would you like a ride to school today?" Mom asked as I sipped my

coffee.

"Um, I guess." I looked up at her, confused. I had the feeling I was

missing something, but for obvious reasons, I didn't know what they

could've been.

"Okay. Be ready to leave in 5 minutes." She smiled at me and

disappeared upstairs. Following suit, I decided to inquire as to the morning

plans.

"Hey, mom? What's going on?" I asked, right on her heels.

"What do you mean?" She turned around and looked at me.

"I was just wondering if you'd talked to Mr. Petersen yet." I blinked.

"Actually, yes. I'm dropping you off at the school, and then I'm going

to meet with him." She continued towards her bedroom.

Sighing, I walked into my own haven and rummaged through my

bureau for something to wear. It should've been easy. I had more clothes than I knew what to do with. But as any teenager can attest to, I couldn't decide for the life of me.

"Come on. We're going to be late." Mom peeked in as I pulled a tank top over my head.

"I'm coming. I'm coming." I grumbled mockingly.

"Yeah, yeah." She grumbled back with a smirk.

The car ride was silent with the exception of the radio. I didn't know what to say, and mom wasn't providing much conversation of her own. Should I ask questions? Or should I wait and see what was to happen? Could I trust mom to handle my affairs in my best interest? Did she actually begin to consider my perspective, or was still she the 'adult that knew better than the child?'

It doesn't matter now. I thought to myself. *I'm already at school. I guess I have no choice but to trust her.*

"Have a nice day, dear." Mom smiled at me.

"You too. Good luck mom." I smiled back.

"I love you."

"Love you, too." As I closed the door, I stood there and watched her slowly drive away. The administration building was across the street, but it seemed so far away. For some reason, I didn't want my mom to leave my side. I knew she was the only person I could place any amount of trust in. Is that sad or what?

Making my entrance, I took my usual seat in homeroom. I watched as the attendant passed out the slips. As usual, I received one. This time, it was orange again.

Damn it! I fumed. *What do they want with me now?*

I had no desire to see Jeannette in the guidance department today, tomorrow, or any other day for that matter. She didn't understand, and just like every other adult, I didn't think it was possible to make her understand my plight.

With a sigh, I trudged to my destiny.

It won't be that bad. Maybe she'll be a good distraction. Superego smiled.

Maybe she'll give my girl a headache with her constant smiles. Id rolled her eyes.

Do you always have to be such a bitch? Superego snapped.

Do you always have to be 'Little Miss Golden Ray of Sunshine'? Id snapped back.

"Good morning." The receptionist smiled at me.

Hollowly, I returned her smile as I dropped the pass on her desk.

"I'll let Ms. Benton know you're here." Picking up the phone, I directed my attention to the atrocious paintings once again.

"Good morning." Jeanette peeked her head out from around the same corner. "Shall we?"

I followed her in silence as we walked back to her office.

"So, how was your weekend?" Jeannette smiled at me as she sat down in her seat. This time, she was wearing a baby blue turtleneck with navy dress pants on.

"It was okay." I shrugged.

"What did you do?" She asked, taking out a pad and paper.

"Played solitaire and hung out with my mom."

She jotted down my words and nodded. "I see."

I looked around the room, trying to figure out where she had cleverly hidden the radio. While it wasn't playing today, finding it was better than dealing with her.

"So, would you like to finish our discussion from last week?" She asked.

"Huh?" Startled, my head whipped around to face hers.

"Last week, I asked you what had upset you so much that your mom called us. She's really concerned about you." Batting her eyes, she smiled at me.

"I don't know." I shrugged.

"You don't know why your mom would be concerned about you?" She furrowed her eyebrows at me but the smile on her face gave away her playful nature.

"No."

"Do you and your mom argue?" She asked, scribbling on the notepad.

"Mom and I always fight." I shrugged.

"About what?"

"Everything."

"And why do you suppose that is?" Thoughtfully, she rested the pen near the corner of her mouth.

"I don't know." I shrugged.

"Do you think she's not listening, or maybe she doesn't understand?" Jeannette pulled the corners of her mouth upwards.

"I guess." I nodded slightly.

"What doesn't your mom understand?" She tilted her head to the left.

"Everything." I shrugged.

"Well, I'm trying to understand. Can you explain it to me?" She smiled again. This time, her smile wasn't as annoying to me.

I shrugged again. There were so many things bothering me. Where did I start to sift through all of the stress and begin?

"Last time, you said you didn't have any friends." She looked at me.

"I don't." My voice came out quiet, barely above a whisper.

"That's got to be lonely."

"It sucks." I shrugged.

"Why do you suppose you don't have any friends?" She asked, scribbling down our conversation.

"I don't know."

"Does it bother you?" She asked.

"Not really. It used to, but not anymore."

"What bothers you now?"

"They won't leave me alone." I could feel my anger beginning to bubble.

"Who won't?"

"Everyone. The other students, the teachers, my mom…" I trailed off.

"Do they all want the same thing?" She asked.

"What?" I looked at her, bewildered.

"Do the students want the same things as the teachers and as your mom?" She asked.

"No." I shook my head.

"Okay, what do the other students want?"

"Just to give me shit. I mean, crap. I mean, just to be mean." I blurted out. Even though mom wasn't there, I could feel her disappointment emanating from her location.

"Oh, you can swear. It's just the two of us. I won't tell anybody." She winked at me and smiled.

My heart returned the smile. It was nice to finally be able to express myself, regardless if mom disagreed with the way I chose how to.

Maybe she's not as bad as I originally thought. I smirked to myself.

"Oh, come on. It's just us girls." She smiled, nudging my arm with her elbow. "You can dish."

"It's bullshit! They gave me detention for having a cell phone!" I snapped, the tears threatening to run free down my cheeks. My soul jumped at the opportunity to drop any emotional baggage it was forced to carry day by day.

"You poor thing! I didn't mean to upset you!" She exclaimed, wrapping her arms around me. I stiffened at her touch. Who was she? Why was this stranger hugging me?

"Why did they give you detention? Just for having a phone?" She asked, handing me a tissue.

"No. Because they thought I was trying to call somebody. But I wasn't! And they wouldn't listen to me when I said I'd never called anyone before! They didn't listen to me when I said that I never used the cell phone or the house phone!" I accepted the tissue.

"Well, that's not very nice of them." She shook her head.

"No. It's bullshit!"

"So, do you think they were valid?" She asked, raising an eyebrow.

"No." I snapped.

I say slap the bitch and walk out! Id piped up, exuding her own enthusiasm.

And what will that accomplish? Superego snorted. It was apparent that Superego was getting tired of playing "good cop" with Id.

I'm just saying. She keeps asking the same stupid questions over and over, and can't understand why she's getting the same answers over and over! She's annoying! We don't know this bitch! Why does she think we'll open up and talk to her like a bunch of girls at a sleep over? Dumb bitch! Id sneered.

She's trying to talk to us. She's trying to get us to open up and talk about our feelings. She cares. She wants to help but she has no idea what's going on. How can she help if we leave her in the dark? Then how

is she supposed to light the way for us to get out of our own darkness?
Superego pouted.

"Okay. What reasons did they have for giving you detention?" She
asked, scribbling on her pad.

"Which time?" Sarcasm seeped through my words.

"Oh, my! You've had detention more than once?" Her eyes opened
wide, revealing the blue flecks in the background of her corneas. "What
ever for?"

I shook my head. It was taking all of my being not to explode.
Thinking about all the various times I had detention pissed me off.

"Because I leave." I concentrated on my breathing, trying to calm
myself down.

"Do you mean, you leave school?" She asked. I nodded. "How come?"

"Why would I stay? Everyone's giving me crap! The other students
pick fights with me and slam me into lockers. The administration gives me
detention for not doing things their way. It's bullshit!" I snorted.

"Somebody slammed you into a locker?" She asked, her eyes opening
wide once again.

"Yeah. I got hit right here." My index finger ran over the point of impact. I could still feel the scab.

"That's horrible! Are you okay?"

"Yeah, it's pretty much healed now. But I went to the nurses' office for an ice pack, and no one was there. So I went home to get an ice pack, and they gave me detention for not going to the main office! I didn't want to get the bitch in trouble! I just wanted a fricking ice pack!" I shook my head at the administration's logic.

"Did they say why they gave you detention?" She offered me the box of tissues, but I declined. I had successfully grabbed the reins of my angst, or so I had hoped.

"Yeah. They don't like students bullying other students, but they're stupid. They think by having the police here that it's going to stop. But it hasn't stopped!" I shook my head in disapproval.

"Has somebody else bullied you since the police have been here?" She asked, scribbling.

"Oh yeah!" I nodded.

"How many times?" She looked up at me.

"At least two or three."

"Oh my!" It was her turn to shake her head.

"And when they bully you, what do you do?" She asked.

"Nothing." I shrugged.

"Absolutely nothing?" She raised an eyebrow at me.

"Yeah."

"Okay. What else would you like to talk about?" She smiled at me, leaning back in her chair.

"I don't know." I shrugged. I became quiet again.

At least her shoulders are getting a good work out. Superego giggled at her own private joke.

"I have a question." Her smile revealed her top row of teeth.

Leaning my head forward a little bit, I indicated I was listening.

"Do you ever bully anyone?" She asked.

"No." I shook my head adamantly.

"Never?"

"Never."

"Why not? If all the other kids are doing it, why not do it back?" She tilted her head to the right.

"Why would I do it to them? I know it sucks." I squinted my eyes at her.

"What do you mean, you know it sucks?" She asked.

"I know it sucks." I reiterated. "If I don't like how it feels, why I would make someone else feel that way?"

"I don't know, but that's a good point." She nodded in agreement.

"You said you've been bullied since the police have been here. How have people bullied you?" She scribbled down her question on her pad.

"Well, that girl that pushed me into my locker went to trial for gang assault, and she was convicted. While she was in jail, one of her friends put rat poison in my locker..." I began.

"Rat poison?! Oh my goodness!" A shocked expression slapped itself across her face.

"Yeah. And she got in trouble for it." I nodded. "Then there were these girls in my gym class who were calling me a snitch because that girl went to jail."

"And how did that make you feel?"

"Pissed off!"

"Why's that?" She looked up at me.

"It wasn't my decision to send her to jail. Don't get me wrong, she deserved it, but why punish me?" I threw my hands up in the air.

"That's a very sharp perception." She smiled at me. "Were there any more instances?"

"Yeah. That girl's brother threatened to have someone beat me up because I guess she got beat up in jail." I smiled back.

"When was this?"

"Friday."

Her eyes went large, protruding in disbelief. The pen ceased to caress the pad as Jeannette tried to wrap her mind around the severity of what it really meant to be in high school.

"Oh my!" Her favorite expression.

I nodded, emphasizing the seriousness of the situation.

"Did you tell Mr. Mitchell?" She asked, leaning in as if I were telling a campfire story.

"Why would I do that?" I jerked my head back. "It wouldn't do any good. He'd bring Justin down to the office and send him to detention."

"What would you rather Mr. Mitchell do to Justin?" Fervently, she scribbled down his name on the pad.

"I don't know, but I think how he handles things now doesn't cut it." Lifting my right leg, I gently draped it over my left thigh.

"Did you tell your mother?" She asked.

"Yeah. She said she was going to talk to Mr. Petersen again."

"There is certainly a lot of drama! Maybe you should try out for the drama club!" She joked, smiling.

"Mmm, no."

"Why not? Oh yeah, I forgot. You don't want to do any after school activities. May I ask, why not? It's a good way to meet new people. You might even make new friends!"

I blinked. I was unsure of how to respond. Check that. I knew exactly what to say, but I didn't know how to say it without sounding like a complete bitch. I wanted to say, "Fuck that! I hate this place! Why the fuck would I stay longer when I can't stand the time I have to be here?!"

But as my mother always says, "Try to articulate your message in a positive manner. People will be more receptive to what you have to say if you present it positively."

"Let me guess. You don't want to stay after school?" She nudged me.

"No." I shook my head slightly, my left dimple peeking through its hiding place in my cheek.

"I understand. Have you ever thought of joining an organization that has nothing to do with school? Maybe a sport?"

"What?" I crinkled my nose at her. I hated sports. There was a reason I barely participated in gym. The reason being I had to in order to pass it! If I had things my way, I would've sat there playing on a computer all day!

"I'm just trying to think of ways you can get out there and meet new people. Maybe make some friends." She shrugged.

I sat there in silence. It wasn't that I didn't want friends, mind you. It was that I had been alone for so long, that I didn't know if making friends now mattered as much to me as she thought it did, or what the importance was, or if making new friends would impact my life in a significant manner.

"Okay, enough of that. I can see that's getting us nowhere." She smiled at me. "So how did Justin's words make you feel? You said his name was Justin, right?"

"It hurt. A lot."

"Anything else?" She asked.

I shrugged. Id wanted to brag about her idea involving chlorine gas, but I kept my mouth shut. Superego was right. I couldn't admit to wanting to hurt everyone. They'd lock me away as fast as they could.

"It pissed me off." I shrugged.

"I can see why it would upset you." She nodded in understanding. Glancing at her watch, she stood up. "Well, first period is almost over. We'd better get you going to second period. You don't want to be late and get detention!" A smile graced her face.

"Yeah." I said.

"Real funny." Id rolled her eyes.

"Hey. She's nice to us. Why don't you give her a chance and be nice to her?" Superego grumbled.

"I'll see you soon." She led me back to the receptionist, where I received a hall pass.

"Have a nice day!" She smiled.

"You too." I walked across the hall to the cafeteria where my second period study hall was to commence shortly. Dropping the pass in front of the attendant, I walked to my seat and took out a sheet of paper.

November 4, 2006   8:44am

So I saw the guidance department again. This time, it wasn't so bad. I don't know why, but the first time really bugged me. Her name is Jeannette, and she's really friendly. She asks a lot of questions though, like why don't I have any friends and do I want to join an after school activity to make friends. If I haven't had any friends up before, what difference would it make now? I don't know why it seems like she wants to know everything. I hope mom is having luck with Mr. Petersen. I'll probably call her at lunch time and see how that went. I'm curious as to what these people think they can do to solve this. These kids aren't going to stop bullying me. It's going to take something drastic to make them stop! Something like chlorine gas. Hahaha! I wouldn't. But seriously, maybe I should. I don't know. If I can find a way to make this stop without hurting anyone, then I'll take it.

Chapter 9

Time is one of those relative terms that people throw around. Sometimes, they are referring to an appointment that must be kept. Other times, they are using it as a schedule guideline. One thing remains true no matter how you are referring to time. It always marches forward. It may be slower than you'd like, or too fast, but time marches on.

The clock was so cruel as it taunted me with its slow passing. I ached for my lunch period, for the ability to call my mom. Patience wasn't my strongest suit, and I <u>had</u> to know what Mr. Petersen said about Justin.

Maybe it wouldn't have gone so slowly if I paid attention to what my teachers had to say instead of watching the clock, but like other obsessions, a person can't help themselves. However, destiny has a funny way of altering time.

I was sitting there watching the clock, minding my own business, when Mr. Mitchell walked into my classroom.

"Good morning. I would like to have a word with one of your students." He informed Mrs. Grant.

"Certainly. Which one?" She asked with a smile.

"Ms. Edwards, can you join me in the hall for a moment?" He stared at me, unblinking, unwavering.

I wanted to shrink in my chair until I was visually unobtainable. Everyone was staring at me, wondering what events occurred to trigger such an unsolicited visit. Slowly, I picked my belongings up. With my head down, I followed him to the solitude of the hallways.

"Why didn't you tell me you were having issues with another student?" He asked as soon as the latch of the door had clicked.

I shrugged. I didn't know what to say that would make him happy, and I knew the truth would only exacerbate his negative views of me.

"Well, I received a phone call from Mr. Petersen this morning, and he said that you were having issues with a student in your gym class. Is that true?" Mr. Mitchell placed his fist under his chin, trying to mimic Auguste Rodin's "The Thinker."

I nodded.

"Would you mind telling me about the incident?" He was beginning to sound aggravated by my lack of verbal responses.

"Well, this guy said he was going to have someone beat me up." I looked at the ground, twiddling my toes around on the tile floor.

"Who said that?"

"Justin."

"Justin who?" He asked.

"The cheerleader's brother?" I mimicked his lilt, as if asking a question.

"I will speak to him later. If someone is harassing you, I can't help you if I don't know about it. Why didn't you come to me?" He scolded.

Because you are useless! What the fuck are you going to do? Give them detention?! Ooohh, watch out now. That's really going to make them stop. Dumbass. Id sneered.

Stop that! He's doing the best he can with what he has. Superego snapped.

I shrugged. Again, I didn't know what to say to him. I knew that if he knew how I felt, that he'd be less inclined to "offer his services".

"What days do you have gym?" He shifted his weight to his left side.

"2, 4, and 6." I mumbled.

I always thought it was strange how they scheduled high school. We didn't go by any traditional calendar. We went through a 6 day cycle. Each student had gym and study halls on alternating days. This way, exactly half of the year went to each course.

"Okay. What I'm going to do is switch you to days 1, 3, and 5. Is that okay?" He asked.

I nodded.

"So the next time you have gym will be Wednesday. I will inform your gym teacher of the schedule change. Get back to class."

Turning on my heels, my hand reached for the knob when...

"Oh, and Ms. Edwards?" His voice stopped me in my tracks.

"Yes?" I turned around to look at him.

"This is the last time I will say this. Please come to me if you are having issues with another student. I can't help you if I don't know what's going on. Are we clear?" Mr. Mitchell folded his arms across his chest.

"Yes, sir."

"Good. Have a nice day."

I didn't respond. I just darted into Mrs. Grant's classroom, unintentionally interrupting a presentation.

My cheeks burned as I could feel everyone's eyes on me. I didn't care. I was too preoccupied with the news I had just received.

November 4, 2006 10:13am

So I guess Mr. Mitchell knows about Justin. Mr. Petersen must have told him. Not that I care. Their solution is to switch my gym class. Yeah, because switching my class is going to make him stop! He threatened to have someone beat me up! Are these people stupid? It doesn't matter when I have gym class! If he has someone beat me up, they could beat me up at any time! Not just gym class! These people are so stupid! I can't stand adults! I don't want to be like them when I grow up! This is ridiculous! They don't listen! They have no idea what is really going on! I'm still going to call mom at lunch. I don't think this is a good idea. And if Justin really wants to send someone to fight me, then that's what they're going to get. A fight.

Chapter 10

Pacing a few steps back and forth in front of my locker, I waited for the ringing to be interrupted by a woman's voice.

"Hi, you've reached the voicemail of…" Mom's voice chanted her message. I didn't bother to listen to its entirety. Slamming the phone shut, I angrily threw it into my purse.

"You know you are not supposed to use cell phones during school hours." A woman's stern voice snapped at me from behind. Turning around, there was a woman standing there. I'd never seen her before. She was an ambiguous blob. The only way one could tell she was a woman was the cheap lipstick she chose to wear. She was "fluffy", wearing a sweatshirt and jeans.

"I was just trying to call my mom." I blinked, unsure of what to say.

"Cell phones are not allowed during school hours." She repeated in the same snippy tone.

"It's my lunch." I snipped back.

"Let's see what Mr. Mitchell has to say about it." She headed towards the main office, turning her red tinted mullet over her shoulder to make sure I was following.

Sighing, I slammed my locker shut. Trudging down the hallway, I followed trouble.

"Good morning, Rita." The receptionist greeted the strange woman.

"Crap. It's the 'skip' monitor!" I grumbled to myself. Hearing her name clarified who she was. I had heard the other kids talk about an adult who roamed the halls and the grounds outside of the school to see if anyone was skipping. Her name was Rita, and she would write you up if she caught you.

"This young lady was on her cell phone." She waved her hand in my direction.

"Good morning, Ms. Edwards!" She smiled at me.

"Good morning." I mumbled.

"If you needed to use a phone, why didn't you come and use the phone here?" She asked.

"My mom gave me this phone so that I could call her." I said. I wasn't sure how this situation was going to play out.

"Are you feeling okay?" Her eyebrows furrowed.

"Yea. Mom had a meeting with Mr. Petersen this morning. I just wanted to know how it went." I shrugged the explanation off.

"Ahh. Well unfortunately, Rita's right. Cell phone use is prohibited during school hours, so I'm going to have to inform Mr. Mitchell about this." She picked up the phone.

"Son of a bitch." I gritted my teeth, cursing under my breath.

"He'll see you now." She smiled at me.

Taking a slight breath, my feet darted forward to carry me towards trouble.

"Have a seat," Mr. Mitchell said upon hearing me knock.

As usual, I sat in the seat closest towards the door, furthest away from him.

"I was told you were using your cell phone during school hours. Is that correct?" He looked at me.

I nodded slightly.

"Is there an issue I should be made aware of?" He asked.

"Mom had a meeting with Mr. Petersen this morning. I just wanted to know how it went." I batted my eyes innocently.

"I already spoke to Mr. Petersen this morning. He is the one who authorized you transferring gym classes. The next time you have a question, please come discuss it with me." He spat in his typical monotone frequency.

"Yes, sir." I nibbled on the inside of my bottom lip, waiting for this torturous meeting to be over.

"Unfortunately, I'm going to have to give you detention. You were informed prior to today that cell phone use will not be permitted under any circumstances. With that said, I am assigning you three days lunch detention beginning today. When is your lunch?" He scribbled down something on a notepad sitting in front of him.

"Fifth period." I clenched my jaw, trying not to show how upset I was.

"It's fifth period now. Well, that won't work. You can start tomorrow. How does that sound?" Mr. Mitchell looked up at me.

How is it supposed to sound, asshole? Why the fuck would she be enthusiastic about detention? Id snapped.

She broke one of the school's rules. There are rules in place for a reason, and there are consequences for when a person breaks them. Superego countered.

They give her detention for NOT calling her mother and leaving. They give her detention for trying to call her mother. She can't fucking win! Id shrieked. *Damned if you do, damned if you don't.*

"Okay." I grumbled. I wasn't going to lie and pretend to be happy about receiving lunch detention.

"Go to lunch. Make sure you report to detention tomorrow." Tearing the piece of paper off of the pad, he stood up. Following suit, I darted out the office before anyone could say anything else.

I stormed down the hallway in the direction of my locker. My vision blurred as the anger flowed through my veins, taking over all logical thought.

That's bullshit! I fumed with each step. *They bitch at me for NOT using a phone to call my mom. Then they bitch at me for using a phone to call my mom*! What the fuck? *I can't win*!

I say shoot them. These bastards just want to be in control. They don't care if the rules don't make sense or contradict each other. They just have to be in control. Id egged on my anger, hoping I'd snap.

They're not trying to contradict themselves. They just want to maintain order. That's how they believe they can keep everyone the safest. Superego countered, trying to diffuse my anger.

"It's bullshit!" I yelled down the hall. Hearing my voice echo off the walls startled me, causing me to stop in my tracks.

Haha! Id yelped with laughter.

Get a move on before Rita comes back. Superego whispered.

Are you really going to take their hypocrisy? Id smirked.

What hypocrisy?! *They're trying to establish and maintain order*! Superego retorted.

Come on. Slip out the door and walk home. Who's going to notice?
Rita's going to be walking around the halls, making sure that no one is
skipping. If she's indoors, she can't be outdoors, can she? Id urged.

Don't say that. She'll get in more trouble if she does that. Besides, she
has classes this afternoon. If she leaves, she'll be interrupting her
education!"= Superego scolded.

And what kind of an education is she getting now? There's way too
many distractions. There's detention and the other kids threatening to hurt
her and some do... Id trailed off.

"You know what? You're absolutely right! What kind of a fucking
education am I getting?! This is bullshit!" I ripped open my locker and
threw my book bag inside. "I'm done. I'm not dealing with this crap. It
may work for other people, but it doesn't work for me." I took one last
look around the halls to make sure the coast was clear, and I slipped out
the side doors.

It was brisk outside, but my ire kept me toasty the entire stomp home. I
didn't realize I had "tunnel vision" until I suddenly arrived on my back
porch.

Looking up, I felt my anger subside as my safety came into focus. My heart froze in anticipation of trouble. I realized that allowing Id to take momentary control would come back to haunt me, regardless if I thought her point was valid.

"Crap." I spat as I walked inside. It was too late. Sixth period already began, so I couldn't walk back to school. I had to live with my decision. Even though I had changed my mind, it was too late.

Let's go sit down and think about this. I'm sure we can figure something out. Superego cooed.

Yeah, like how to get the shit we need to kill everyone! Id grinned.

Guilt escorted me upstairs to my computer, directing me to sit and think about the crimes I had committed.

November 4, 2006 11:57am

Son of a bitch! I got more lunch detention! I hate that asshole! Mr.

Mitchell told me to call my mom if I was having problems instead of

leaving school and walking home. I called her because Justin threatened to

have someone beat me up, and they give me detention for calling her! I

can't fucking win! How am I supposed to get through my classes and do

my work if everyone keeps pissing me off?! Something's got to change,

because I'm going to snap before the year is over at this rate! I'm going to

try to call mom again. Hopefully, she answers this time.

Chapter 11

I closed my eyes, taking in several deep breaths with the phone in my trembling left hand. I tried to think about what I wanted to say, and what she would say in response to the things I said.

My heart thumped against its bony frame as I dialed mom's number with a shaky hand. I counted the rings as I waited for her to pick up.

"Hello?" Her soothing cheeriness felt like a warm blanket around my soul.

"Hi mom." I smiled slightly.

"Hey, Fang. What's up?" I could hear the smiled being returned in her voice.

"How did the meeting with Mr. Petersen go?" I asked.

"Fine. He thinks you should be transferred out of that gym class." She informed me.

"That's it?" I blurted.

"Yes, that's it. Were you expecting something else?" She teased.

Uh yeah, actually. Because if Justin said he was going to have someone kick my girls' ass, he could have someone do it at any time. Not just gym class. What the fuck y'all going to do to solve that problem? Id snapped.

"I was just wondering." I shrugged.

"Aren't you supposed to be in class?" Mom's voice resonated with concern.

I went silent.

"Robin Rachael!" Mom snapped. "What is going on?"

"Nothing." I snapped back.

"Why aren't you in class?" Her words resumed their cross tone.

"I got detention." I grumbled.

"What? Why?!"

"I tried to call you during lunch to see how the meeting went, and they gave me lunch detention!" I whined.

"Oh my goodness. I'm on my way home. Make sure you're ready when I get there." I heard a click, and the phone line went dead.

"Son of a bitch." I threw the phone on the bed. Sighing, I spun around in my chair to face my computer. I had a very limited amount of time to figures things out before mom came home, and I knew when she did, things were going to get a lot more complicated.

November 4, 2006   12:08pm

Son of a bitch! Mom's pissed off now because I walked home from school. I tried to explain it to her, but she hung up on me. What the fuck am I going to do now?! Nobody will listen to me! I got to figure something out, and quick. I'm NOT going back to that school. Not today, and probably not tomorrow! I can't deal with always getting in trouble and always being in detention! I spend more time in Mr. Mitchell's office and in detention than in class! At this rate, I might as well just drop out!

Chapter 12

As the seconds ticked by, the logical processes in my brain began to shut down. Things swirled around in my mind, becoming cloudy with emotions. My breathing became labored, shallow, and my hands suddenly went cold. What was I going to do? How was I supposed to "fix" this? Was there anything I could say that would make Mr. Mitchell and my mom understand? How could they think I was a bad kid when I didn't do anything wrong? Why was Mr. Mitchell always out to get me? <u>Was</u> Mr. Mitchell out to get me?

I paced around my room trying to analyze the situation, but to no avail. I was just "the child". I had no say in this situation, or any other situation that would arise.

If I stay, Mom will come home and take me back to school. And I'll probably get in detention for missing 6th period. I thought to myself.

Well dear, there are rules. You must obey the rules. They're in place to maintain order, to keep everyone safe. Superego's soothing voice did nothing to ease the sting of her words.

That's bullshit! Id yelled. *The rules are in place to keep everyone safe, but what happens when one of the rules causes more harm than good?*

You need to think of everyone. Of course all of the rules aren't going to apply to everyone, but it is important that rules be maintained for the general good.

The general good. What a load of crap! Id sneered.

You need to stay and face the consequences. Superego scolded.

Fuck that! Fight the system! Id yelled.

Stay.

Go.

Stay!

Go!

I couldn't take it anymore. My brain hadn't provided me with any feasible solutions, so my body took over. As autopilot commanded my physical functions, I found myself running. I had no idea where I was going.

I could see the houses in my neighborhood whizzing past me as I heard my sneakers thudding against the pavement. My heart pounded louder than thunder in my ears as a raspy pant rapidly escaped my lips.

You should turn around and face the consequences! Superego's worry emanated prominently.

You should try out for the track team! *Damn girl*! *Look at you go*! Id laughed at her own joke.

I could see trees thickening around me, and slowed my desperate run to a moderate trot. Looking around, I noticed that the pavement had given way to flora. Stopping short of a fallen tree branch, I pressed my right hand into an ache that had appeared in my side. It burned with each breath, and the idea of using the fallen branch as a pose for my derriere suddenly seemed very appealing.

Shifting my weight repeatedly side to side, I tried to distract my emotional attention to something physical as I tried to get comfortable. I could feel the guilt rising up in my chest, begging me to go back home and resolve this.

"No!" I said aloud. "I am not a bad kid, and I am <u>not</u> going to be treated as one!"

The guilt didn't waver. Instead, it remained steadfast, threatening to increase if I didn't comply with its unreasonable demands.

"What am I going to do now?" I asked myself. "Nobody's going to find me here. Hell, I don't even know where I am! How is anyone else going to find me?"

Closing my eyes, I tried to crawl out from under the severity of the circumstances using logical thought as my shovel.

"Okay. Why did I run? That's simple. I didn't want to go back to school. Why don't I want to go back to school? Because Mr. Mitchell gave me detention for doing something he told me to do! I understand that part, but I don't understand what I'm supposed to do now." I mumbled to myself. Focusing on my breathing, I tried to sift through the remainder of my thoughts and feelings.

You need to go back and face this, Superego urged. *It's only going to get worse the more you delay it.*

So she can get in more trouble?! *I don't fucking think so*! *That's what's going to happen, and you know it*! *These adults don't care how she feels*! *They'll condemn her for breathing*! Id snorted.

Sinking my head into my heads, I knew they were both right. The longer I waited to face this, the worse the punishment was going to be. But in my mind, I hadn't done anything worth getting in trouble for! Taking a few deep breaths, I wondered about what was going to happen. I knew it wasn't going to be good, but I couldn't help wondering if there <u>was</u> something that I could do about it. If I fought back, would it make things better, or worse?

Why don't you go find out? Come on, give it a shot. Fight back. Those bullshit rules were put in place to protect the students, but they're hurting you. Are you going to let them keep hurting you or are you going to fight back? Id egged me on.

They are not blasphemous! Those rules were designed to keep everyone safe! And don't act like the faculty is deliberating trying to hurt her because you know that's not true! Superego snapped.

Are you blind or just stupid? Every time she goes to school, she unknowingly breaks a rule and gets detention! How does that make her feel? Like she's a bad kid! They're ostracizing her, turning her into a bad kid! Id snapped back.

Don't be ridiculous! They are not turning her into a bad kid! Superego snorted.

Are you sure about that? If she thinks she's going to get in trouble for every little thing she does, then sooner or later, she's going to purposefully be bad. Then that little idea of mine won't seem like such a bad one. Id's left cheek pulled up in an arrogant smirk.

She wouldn't use chlorine gas on everyone. She's too good a girl for that. Superego rolled her eyes.

Everyone may think she's a good girl, but if she thinks she's a bad one, then what does it matter to her? Her right cheek pulled up.

Superego opened her mouth to reply, but no sound came out. She knew Id had a point, so she decided against whatever feeble retort she was going to try to use.

That's a good girl. Now are you going to fight with me to save our girl, or are you going to let those ignorant adults shred her to pieces? Id retained her smirk.

Fine. What do you think will rectify this situation? Superego sighed.

Like I said, we need to fight back. Mr. Mitchell told her that she was only allowed to use her cell phone during lunch and not school hours. She did exactly what he said, and he gave her detention. So we need to remind that son of a bitch that she did exactly what he told her to, and that he can't be giving her detention every fucking week! Id pumped her fist.

Do you have to curse so much? You sound atrocious when you talk like that! Superego crinkled her nose in disgust.

Hell yea! Now let's go whoop some ass!

Taking in a deep breath, I picked myself up off of the fallen branch and decided to confront my troubles. Brushing off any flora that had possibly attached itself to my derriere, I headed back in the direction I remembered coming from. I wasn't 100% sure of what I was going to say. I just knew that I desperately wanted to fight this. I wanted to let the adults know that they were wrong, and I was right. I wasn't a bad kid and I didn't want to always be in trouble! In fact, the only thing I wanted was to be left alone. I left everyone alone, and that's all I wanted from them.

Once the flora gave way to pavement, I saw the outskirts of my neighborhood. I knew I passed these houses every time I walked home, so I followed the rows until I was close enough to my house to see mom's car sitting in the driveway. What I didn't see was mom sitting in the car until I had already passed it.

"Robin Rachael! Where have you been?!" She screamed at me.

Jumping, I spun around. I could see mom didn't look too thrilled that I hadn't been home when she got here.

"I just went for a walk." I shrugged. I couldn't explain what made me run in the first place, so I didn't bother trying to.

"Get in the car. I'm taking you back to school." Mom climbed back in the car, slamming her door.

"I don't want to go back." I mumbled to myself, but complied with her irate demand.

I hadn't even put my seatbelt on before mom threw the car into gear. Catching myself against the dash, I looked incredulously at her.

"What is going on with you?!" She spat.

"Nothing." My lone word lingered in exasperation.

"You can't just leave school when you feel like it! Did something happen today?" Gripping the steering wheel, her knuckles slightly paled.

"I tried calling you at lunch to find out how the meeting with Mr. Petersen went, and Mr. Mitchell gave me detention for using the phone you gave me on my lunch break!" I spat back.

"If Mr. Mitchell said no cell phones..." Mom began.

"No. He said no cell phones during school hours. That's why I waited until my lunch break to call you." I interjected. The logic of the scenario was so clear to me, and yet it seemed to elude everyone else.

"Your lunch break is still considered to be during school hours, is it not?" Her irate tone grew, reflecting in her treatment of the pedals.

"He told me that I could use it during lunch, but <u>not</u> school hours!" I snapped. "And I wasn't calling anybody! I was calling you to see how your meeting with Mr. Petersen went."

Jerking the car to a stop in the parking lot, Mom turned and looked at me.

"What is going on? Talk to me." Her voice was quieter, calmer, but her eyes flickered at an eerie fear that loomed just beneath the surface.

"I hate school. I hate the other students, and I hate the adults. Everyone always gives me crap. Everyone. And when I tell the adults, I get in trouble. When the other students give me more crap, I get in trouble. Nothing I do is ever good enough! I just want to be left alone!" I ranted, exhaling loudly.

"So why don't we go discuss this with Mr. Mitchell?" Mom tilted her head to the right, her eyes pleading with me for compliance.

"Mr. Mitchell isn't going to do anything! He gives me crap just as bad as the kids do! He's always giving me detention." I dropped my shoulders as if to say "I give up."

"Well, we have to find a solution to this! You cannot keep skipping school whenever you feel like it!" Her snippy tone had returned.

"It's not that I want to skip school, mom! I just want to be left alone! By everybody! I just want to go to school and do my work! I don't want to talk to anybody! I don't want anybody to talk to me! I just want to be left alone!" I snipped back.

"Well, the real world doesn't revolve around what you want! Sometimes, you have to do what makes other people happy because you don't have a choice! Do you think I want to be taking time off of work to come take you back to school?! Nooo, but if I don't, you won't go back! Grow up!" Mom yelled.

"Fuck you!" I yelled back, pushing through the car door. Slamming it behind me, I started running. I wanted to get away from her, from everyone whose ignorance made my high school experience impossible.

I could hear Mom's car revving up behind me, frantically trying to catch me before I detoured to an area it couldn't follow.

"Get back in the car!" Mom rolled down the window a smidge to scream at me.

I slowed in my tracks, walking backwards to face her. "Why?" I fumed, glaring at her.

"I have to get back to work! You have to get back to school!"

"So go! No one's stopping you!" I turned around, showing off my back to her.

"Robin Rachael!" She snapped.

"What!" I screamed, turning around.

"Get in this damn car!" She slapped the steering wheel, trying to alleviate some of her frustrations.

I stopped moving. Hearing my mom curse distracted me from my own anger. I couldn't think of anything to say, so I just stared at her.

"Please. Get in this car. I'm sorry I yelled at you." Mom looked at me.

"I don't want to go back to school," I repeated softly.

"I know. How about we go home and talk about what's going on." She looked at me with pleading eyes.

Go with her. Maybe the two of you can find a resolution, Superego urged.

Bullshit! It's a scam! She's trying to get you back in the car so she can take you to school! Don't listen to her! Id cautioned.

I was so confused. I knew I had a second to make a decision, but I had no idea which one would be the best choice. On the one hand, she was mad at me and had already commanded me to get in the car, stating I was going back to school. On the other hand, she's my mother. She'd never lied to me previously. Then again, we've never fought like this before. Could I still trust her, or had things taken an irreparable turn for the worse?

Against Id's expressed concerns, I hesitantly climbed into the passenger seat. Every muscular movement felt extreme, as if time had slowed down.

You're going to regret this. Id hissed.

Give her mom some credit. You don't know what's going to happen. Maybe everything will work out. Superego frowned at her counterpart.

"What is going on?" Mom asked, slamming her foot on the gas.

"I told you. I tried to call you during lunch, and Mr. Mitchell gave me detention." I repeated.

"And I told you. If Mr. Mitchell said no cell phones during school hours, then you can't use it during lunch! Do I need to take it away?" She snapped.

"Go ahead." Fishing it out of my purse, I tossed it in her lap.

"Then what are you going to do if something happens?" She asked facetiously.

What the hell do you care? It's not like you're there when something happens. You side with them. You think I deserve this shit. I thought bitterly to myself.

"Well?" She tapped the steering wheel with her fingers.

I just shrugged.

"Well, we have to do something! You can't keep leaving school when you feel like it, and I can't miss work!" Mom took a sharp right, and my body strained against the seatbelt to stay in place.

Honey, talk to her. Explain things to her, because it seems like she genuinely doesn't understand. Superego whispered.

Yeah. Explain to her how she's being a bitch! Explain to her that if those mother fuckers don't <u>back off</u> and quit chastising you like you are a bad girl, then you're going to be a bad girl!" Id spat in retort.

Violence isn't the answer. Superego hissed.

Neither is inaction. Id hissed back.

"Are you just going to sit there, or are you going to answer me?" Mom poked my shoulder.

"Ow." I furrowed my eyebrows, rubbing the spot furiously. "What?"

"What do you suggest we do? Because you can't keep missing school and I can't be missing work." The decibel level of her voice was a lot lower, but there was still an emotionally urgent tone.

"I don't know." My own urgent tone came out, desperately seeking solace from this circular argument.

"I don't know isn't going to solve anything." Mom pulled into our driveway, slightly renewing my faith in the latest kept promise. "How about we go inside and talk about this?"

"Okay." Mechanically I exited the car and headed inside, unfazed by mom brushing past me. Instead, I welcomed the opportunity to follow and flopped down on the opposite side of the couch from her.

"Why did you leave school today?" Mom asked, folding her arms across her chest.

"I told you. I tried to call you during lunch and Mr. Mitchell gave me detention for using the cell phone. But it doesn't matter now because you can have it back." I snipped, folding my arms to assert my own anger.

"Didn't you say that Mr. Mitchell said no cell phones during school hours?" Mom asked, shifting in the cushions.

"That's why I waited to call at lunch." I crossed my right leg over my left.

"And isn't lunch during school hours?" Mom nodded her head forward an inch, pushing out her words.

"Yeah, but I wasn't interrupting any of my classes. That's why I waited until lunch. It's no big deal if I call you during my lunch." I leaned on the arm of the couch, feeling the metal support beam gently prod my ribcage.

Mom shook her head and sighed. "You just don't get it, do you? I swear, Robin. I don't know how you can be so stupid about this."

Her words slapped me viciously in the face, immediately exacerbating my ire towards her. Being blinded by my emotional response left me at a loss for words, so I just glared at her.

"Do you understand that if Mr. Mitchell said no cell phones during school hours, then that includes lunch?" She blinked at me.

"Sure. Whatever." My words were short and sharp as my mind delivered them with part of my internal bile.

Who's she calling stupid? I say smack her! Id yelled, bracing for a fight.

Don't smack her. You'll only make things worse. Superego frowned.

Fuck that! Smack the bitch! Id remained in a pouncing stance.

If you two can't reach a compromise, then I suggest you walk away from the situation until both of you have calmed down. Superego tried to appeal to my sense of reason. Smart move, because it worked.

Fuck you, you stupid bitch. I thought bitterly as I stood up.

"Where are you going?" Mom asked, surprised.

"To my room." I mumbled through gritted teeth. I stormed out of the room, blindly following my rage to isolation.

"We're not done talking though!" She called after me.

I tuned out her ignorance, concentrating on my computer. The things I could do with it, the places I could escape to, was worth any retaliation. I no longer cared about what my mother thought. As far as I was concerned, she was with them, the stupid masses of adults who thought they knew better. From now on, it was up to me to fix things. I was completely on my own.

November 4, 2006 2:17pm

Stupid bitch! I am getting so sick of everyone! Now my mom thinks I'm stupid! She actually called me stupid! I tried to call her during lunch to find out how her meeting with Mr. Petersen went, and Mr. Mitchell gave me detention. So now, I'm the stupid one! Whatever. I gave her back the phone. She can have it. I won't call anyone for help. If someone's giving me crap, then I'll just leave. And when they get pissed off because I don't tell them, oh well. What the fuck are they going to do about it? All they do is bitch at me anyways, even when I don't do anything wrong. And they call me stupid. Um, hello! If I'm not bothering anyone, and I mind my own business, then why am I always getting in trouble? Stupid fucking adults! Keep getting in my face! Keep screaming at me and giving me detention! See how far that gets you! See what happens! If you mother fuckers don't <u>back off</u>, then don't fucking complain when I snap! When all you sons of bitches are hurting, don't fucking ask me why!

Chapter 13

Mindlessly I stared at the solitaire screen, completely unaware of how quickly time was elapsing. With thoughtless repetition, I kept clicking the mouse and moving the cards.

"Who is she calling stupid? At least I'm listening to her. No one is listening to me!" I grumbled to myself.

I don't think you're stupid. I think you were miscommunicating, but I don't think you're stupid. Superego offered a half smile.

I hate to say it, but the bitch is right. You're not stupid. They're stupid. It's this fricking easy. You don't bug anyone, and everyone bugs you. You leave everyone alone, and they won't leave you alone. You never cause trouble, and they always bring trouble to your door. You're not a bad kid. They're just trying to make you out to be one. Id put in her two cents.

You forgot the most important thing, Id. You're right. She's not a bad kid. But nobody is telling her she's a good kid. So if all she is hearing is that she's bad, she's going to eventually believe it. And we can't let her do that. She is a good kid, despite what everyone else thinks. Superego stressed.

Well I don't hear anyone telling her she's a good kid except for us. Id said.

That's not going to do a whole lot of good since we're her subconscious. She may know we're here, but she can't exactly hear us. Superego scolded. *We need to remind other people that she's a good kid. They don't need to constantly praise her but they do need to stop calling her a bad kid, especially if she's a good one."*

I say we let them know how it feels to be told they're bad. Let's hurt them and not tell them why. Then we can flip out on them when they're sitting there say, 'Why? Why did you hurt us?' Dumbasses. Like it's that hard to fucking figure this shit out! Id sneered.

"I just wish everyone would leave me alone." I could feel the vice around my heart squeeze, and tears welled to the surface.

I heard a knock at my bedroom door, and I quickly used my sleeve to erase the evidence of pain from my face.

"Yeah." I barked at the door.

"You ran off before we could finish talking." Mom spoke gently, peering from around the edge of the door.

I rolled my eyes. I couldn't think of a nice way to say, *Fuck you, you stupid bitch*." So I kept my mouth shut.

"If you have more to say, you're welcome to say it. I'll listen to you." I said, waving her in.

"Do you think I'm not listening to you? Because I am." Mom sat down on the edge of my bed.

"I didn't say that, did I?" My words were still sharp, and emanated from my mouth with a bit of a sting.

"Well, I'm listening." She crossed her legs, leaning her elbows on her knees. The mouse stopped clicking, and I slowly turned to look her in the face.

"Go ahead dear." She waved, indicating it was my turn to speak.

I just stared at her like a deer caught in a pair of headlights. The words swirled around in my brain just out of reach. I struggled to grasp them, and organize them into something tangible, but every time I tried, I kept barely missing.

"Well?" She asked impatiently.

"Hang on. I'm thinking." Taking a deep breath, I knew I had a vague notion of what my true feelings were. I also knew that my words weren't going to come out right. But what the hell. I was willing to give it a shot.

"Okay. What would you like to know?" I asked.

"Is there anything you'd like to say?" Mom repeated.

"Yeah. I don't know why everyone is being so mean to me. I don't bother anybody. I just go to school and do my work. I don't cause trouble.

So why can't people just leave me alone?" The corners of my mouth pulled downward slightly.

"Honey, Mr. Mitchell has a school to run. There are rules in place for a reason. Everybody has to follow those rules. When everyone follows the rules, Mr. Mitchell can run the school more efficiently." Mom tilted her head to the right.

Did you hear her ask to break the rules? No. You're not listening to her. Didn't you just say that you'd listen to her? You're not. And you called her a stupid bitch, when who's really being stupid. Open up your ears! Id snapped. *What did my girl say? She said she doesn't like being bothered. She said everyone is bothering her. She said she doesn't talk to anybody, and she just wants to be left alone."*

"Mom! I'm not saying I want to break the rules. I'm just saying I want to be left alone." I sighed.

"Is somebody else giving you a hard time?" She furrowed her brows at me.

I snorted. "Yeah."

"Who?"

"Mr. Mitchell!"

"Oh, Robin…" Mom rolled her eyes at me. Clenching my jaw, I decided that this conversation was over. She wasn't listening to me, as she claimed she would. This was nothing more than an exercise in futility.

"Is anybody giving you a hard time?" Mom asked.

I just stared at her, with no intention of replying.

Mom sighed and stood up. "Well, when you feel like talking, come find me." With that, she walked out of the room.

I stormed over to the door and slammed it shut. I was so tempted to punch it, but I thought the noise would alarm mom. And I wasn't in the mood to "talk" to her. So I turned to the only source I could rely on for comfort.

November 4, 2006   8:49pm

Son of a bitch! Mom came in and tried to talk to me again. But she's not

listening! She acts like I'm the one who doesn't get it! Whatever! All I

want is to be left alone! I don't want to deal with Mr. Mitchell always

giving me detention. I don't want to deal with Mr. Fout being an ass to

me. I don't want to deal with the other students threatening to kick my ass.

I just want to be left alone! I swear, they'd better get out of my face! How would they feel if I flipped out and attacked the whole school? Hell, kids all across the county are flipping out. Maybe I should copy them. I wonder if that's why they did what they did.... Well, I'm going to get some sleep. Hopefully, I'll get enough, seeing as how I know Mr. Mitchell is going to want to give me more detention for missing yesterday afternoon. I'll see if mom will write me a note. I doubt it, but it's worth a try. This has definitely been the day from hell...

Chapter 14

I stared into the mirror, and I couldn't recognize the foreign entity staring back at me. Her skin was pale, with tear stains running down the length of her cheeks. Her eyes seemed glassy, almost as if she was emotionally vacant. It broke my heart to see what had become of me. Was this as bad as things would get, or was there worse to come?

Letting out a deep sigh, I stepped into the shower. I could feel the hot steam floating up around me, and I allowed the warmth of my surroundings to transport me. I didn't want to think about the meeting with Mr. Mitchell or upcoming detention or the fight with my mother. I wanted to leave it all behind, and just be happy for once.

"Are you going to school, or what?" Mom's voice wafted over to me through the foggy blanket.

"Yeah." I called back.

"You'd better get going, or you're going to be late." The same sternness in her voice that I had heard the night before was still there. Somewhere along the way it had picked up a bit of annoyance.

"I'm hurrying." I shouted to no one. Peeking out from behind the curtain, I could see mom had left. Sighing again, I rinsed out the shampoo and parted with my newest "friend."

While I went through the rest of my morning routines, my mind drifted to the nightmare of possibilities that could become my reality. I was pretty sure that Mr. Mitchell was going to ask me where I was yesterday afternoon. How much detention was he going to assign me? Did he even care that I was upset? Since I was with mom, would she give me a note? Did I even want to risk asking her?

"It's worth a shot," I shrugged. Slipping into my boots, I took off in search of the elder one. Using my senses, I followed my nose to the kitchen. Between the coffee and mom's perfume, she did a lousy job of playing hide and seek.

"Hey mom?" I stood a few feet away, wanting to keep the distance between myself and any possible trouble.

"Yes dear." She replied, pouring creamer in her coffee mug.

"I was wondering if maybe you'd right me a note. If not, it's not big deal." I tried to nonchalantly shrug off the seriousness of the discussion.

"For what?" Mom didn't look at me, instead focusing on pushing the cap of her coffee mug.

" Because we came home yesterday." On the outside, I did my best to remain placid. On the inside, I was twitching and freaking out.

"It wasn't my idea for you to come home though. It was yours. Do you really think it's appropriate for me to write you a note excusing you when I was against it?" She looked up at me, sternly glaring at me.

A simple no would've sufficed, I thought to myself as I turned and walked back upstairs.

November 5, 2006 7:43am

So I asked mom, and she won't write me a note. Awesome. Now Mr. Mitchell is going to give me more detention. Whatever. Hopefully, I'll be left alone in detention. I'm just really not in the mood to deal with him. I just want to be left alone.

Chapter 15

The only thing on my mind was time as I scurried away from my computer desk. I didn't need to be late to school. That would give them another excuse to give me more detention.

I grabbed my book bag and flew down the stairs, ready to burst out the door and head out on the trail that would lead me to school. Logic told me that my mother had no intentions of leaving me a note, but adolescent hope prompted me to scan the room. I saw nothing on any of the countertops, and with a heavy heart, I began the journey of another long and torturous day.

■■

I looked around at the other lost lemmings in the main office. We were all here for the same reason: We had received the dreaded hall pass in homeroom, and now we were waiting for Mr. Mitchell to hand each of us down his sentencing. No one ever received a not guilty verdict. It was just a matter of determining punishment.

"Ms. Edwards?" Mr. Mitchell called me from his office. Putting on a brave face, I tried not to show my obvious vulnerability.

"It appears that you missed all of your afternoon classes yesterday." His nose was buried in what I presumed to be my file, which appeared to be growing with every visit.

"Sorry." I mumbled.

"I'm sorry too. I'm going to have to assign you ISS." Mr. Mitchell looked up at me.

"And don't forget, you still have three days of lunch detention. How does this sound? Why don't you report to lunch detention today, then 3 days of ISS and we'll call it even?" Mr. Mitchell's smile was hollow.

"Yes sir." I replied, feeling my soul ache.

"Get going to class." With that, I nearly skipped out of his office, desperately trying to escape the cruelty that had become my reality.

I was walking to my first period study hall when I remembered another pass that had found its way to my pocket. It was a pass issued by the guidance department.

Don't go. Id whispered in my ear.

You have to go! They issued you a pass! Superego countered.

Keeping my eyes on the floor, I followed my feet to study hall. I secretly hoped it was going to be quiet, and that I would be left alone. I decided to follow Id's order, not that I was trying to be rebellious. I just wanted to be left alone.

November 5, 2006 8:21am

Awesome. I have three days of ISS now for skipping my afternoon classes yesterday. It's bullshit. I left as soon as Mr. Mitchell yelled at me for doing what he told me to and then he gave me detention. It's not like I left school and went to a party. I went home and mom yelled at me. I got a pass from the guidance department saying they want to see me, but I didn't go. I don't want to talk to anybody right now. I just want to be left

alone. I leave everybody else alone. Why can't they do the same for me?

Chapter 16

All eyes were on me as I stood there, a complete stranger amongst the

group. Scanning the room, I noticed a few of the faces were vaguely

familiar from roaming the halls. I couldn't place any names with faces,

though.

I had felt this feeling my whole life. A stranger in the group, no matter where I went, no matter what I did. I always stood out, and I would always stand out.

"Everyone, this is Robin Edwards. She was in the other gym class, but now she's with us." The gym teacher smiled as she introduced me to the class. Nobody said any form of greetings to me. They just continued to stare at me.

I wanted nothing more than to leap outside of my own skin and crawl away from the gawking eyes. Did they have nothing better to do with themselves than stare at me? Besides, what were they staring for? I was an insignificant speck on their radars of life. What the hell did they care?

Within 5 minutes, I had become nothing more than an unimportant figment in the past as everyone began running around playing dodge ball. This class was more aggressive than my previous one. I had been hit by a ball within the first ten seconds of playing.

My peers kept running around the room, screaming and throwing dodge balls when Ms. Benton walked in. My stomach clenched as she sauntered over to the gym teacher, and both of the adults turned to look at me. I knew this was because I didn't respond to the hall pass that the guidance department sent me this morning.

As Ms. Benton walked back towards the door she waved me over to her, indicating she wanted me to go with her.

"Why didn't you come this morning?" She pouted when I finally caught up with her.

"Sorry," I mumbled. I shuffled my feet in a desperate attempt to match pace with the speeding blonde.

"Is everything okay?" She asked, pushing open a door that led to her office.

"Yeah, I guess." I shrugged, one step behind her.

"Then why didn't you show up?" She pressed, sitting down in her chair.

"I forgot." I looked down at my boots, twiddling my toes.

"Why do I get the feeling that something's wrong?" She furrowed her brows at me.

I shrugged.

"Come on, Robin. You can talk to me." She leaned in, smiling at me.

I could feel the turmoil that I suppressed deep down inside struggle to erupt. I bit my lip, hoping to keep the demons quiet just a little bit longer. Ten years of torture and abuse inflicted by the hands of my peers had filled my soul with enough toxicity to mimic detonating the atom bomb. The only thing that had kept the black ire under control was not dwelling on any of it. Unfortunately, that's exactly what Jeanette wanted to do. She wanted to dwell, to confront, to prod, all of the battle wounds I had acquired.

"Does this have anything to do with Mr. Mitchell?" She asked.

I jerked my head up and stared at her, unblinking.

"Does this have anything to do with that boy threatening you?"

"No."

"Did Mr. Mitchell give you more detention?" She batted her eyelashes at me.

"Yeah." I sighed.

"Whatever for?" Jeanette pouted at me, trying to be sympathetic.

" Because I tried to call my mom during my lunch yesterday. But there's a no cell phone rule. 'You can't use your cell phone during school hours!' " I mockingly waved my hands in the air.

"Why did you try to call your mom?"

"Mom said she was going to talk to Mr. Petersen about Justin threatening me. I just called her to see how the meeting went." I shrugged.

"And Mr. Mitchell gave you detention?" She asked.

"Yeah."

"You don't sound too happy about that." Jeanette opened her desk drawer, retrieving her trusty pen and pad.

"I think its crap," I snorted and rolled my eyes.

"Why's that?" She blinked at me.

"I called my mom during my lunch. It's not like I called her during any of my classes. I waited until I was free. And Mr. Mitchell told me to call her if there was a problem!" I rolled my eyes again.

"Isn't your lunch during school hours?" She asked.

"So if there's no cell phone usage during school lunch, then how the hell am I supposed to call anyone for help if there's a problem?" I snapped.

"Oh dear! I'm not trying to upset you." She patted my leg.

Don't touch her, you stupid bitch! Id snarled.

Stop that! She's only trying to help! Superego spat.

I took in a deep breath, trying to bury my words and feelings. I didn't want to argue with anyone, about anything, anymore. I just wanted to be quiet, to become invisible, and to be left alone.

"Well, how are things going with your mother?" She asked, detecting that she was hitting a nerve.

My heart winced at the answer. The only "friend" I'd ever had growing up, my mother, and I were at odds. It hurt me more to fight with her than anything anybody at school could ever do or say to me. No matter what happened, I could always run to mom. Not anymore, not now. Now, I was truly alone.

I shrugged, my stare sinking to the floor. My vision blurred as my eyes absorbed everything in sight, distancing me from reality.

"Awww, is that bad?" She leaned in to hug me. I remained motionless and detached as her hands caressed up and down my back, choosing to silently lick my souls' wounds instead like an animal in hiding.

"Talk to me. What's going on?" She put her hands on my shoulder, tucking her head low enough to catch visualization.

"Just fighting." I whispered, trying not to let my mind focus on events that had transpired between us.

"What about?"

"Same shit, different day." I sighed.

"I see." She reached for the box of tissues and offered me one. I plucked one from the box, not wanting to be rude. "It sounds like you're going through a lot. Does it always feel like that?"

Duh! She's 14! Of course it feels like that! Id rolled her eyes.

Shut up! She's trying to help, which is more than I can say for you! Superego wrinkled her nose.

I did offer to help! I'm the one that came up with the idea of using chlorine gas on everyone and showing them how it feels to hurt and you don't know why people are doing it to you! Id retorted.

Yeah, that's a great idea. If it's so great, then why hasn't she done it yet? Superego asked.

Shut the fuck up! You're on her side! Id yelled, referring to Jeanette.

I'm not on anybody's side. I just want what's best for Robin. Don't you? Superego countered.

Of course I do, but I don't think talking to someone is what she needs right now. I think she needs to be left alone. I think if people keep bugging her, she's going to snap. And they're going to wonder why. Id replied.

I disagree. I think she needs to express how she feels, and not bottle it up. I think if she talks about it and lets some of her feelings go, then she'll feel better about things. Superego said.

We'll see. Id stared at her.

Yeah. We'll see. Superego smiled.

"Kind of." I shrugged.

"Kind of? What exactly does 'kind of' mean?" She crinkled her nose at me in a smile.

"Feels like no matter what I do, it's wrong." I said slowly, trying to properly articulate my feelings.

"Aww, don't say that. You're not always wrong." Jeanette smiled.

"Yeah I am." I said sadly.

"Give me one instance." She folded her arms.

"Everything." I said.

"Like what?" She insisted.

"Everything!" The sudden influx of memories from the past decade whizzed through my mind at deafening speeds. "Every little thing I do is bad! I always get in trouble, no matter who does what! I can never do anything right! If I don't say anything, I get in trouble! If I say something, I get in trouble! Ahhhhhhh!" I screamed.

"Oh, my!" She jumped back in her seat.

"Mother fucker, why can't everyone just leave me alone?!?" I curled up in a ball, beginning to cry.

"Oh sweetie…" She wrapped her arms around me, futilely trying to console me.

"No!" I screeched through my knees. "I'm not a bad kid! Leave me alone! I don't do anything to anyone! I don't deserve it! Leave me the fuck alone! How would they like it if I hurt them?!" The words tumbled out before my brain had a chance to filter it. Immediately, I regretted letting them be heard. I knew exactly what Jeanette would think of them, how she would take them.

Good one, slick. Id rolled her eyes.

Shut up! Now she's really in trouble! Everyone's going to think she's going to blow up the school or something! They might lock her away! Superego fretted.

An ice cold chill ran up my spine as the room went unusually quiet. My heart sounded like thunder ticking by the seconds. I closed my eyes tightly, wishing I could disappear. Fear manipulated my extremities like a marionette with ease.

We sat there, rocking in silence, knowing precious time was slipping by. Jeanette kept whispering things like, "it'll be alright" and "don't worry about it", but I couldn't shake the feeling that things were only going to get worse.

"How about you sit tight for a minute while I go get us some water?" She leaned out of the hug, smiling at me.

I nodded slowly, peering at her from behind my fetal cocoon.

"I'll be right back." With that she walked out the door.

That was a mistake. You should've gone with her. Id shook her head.

Why? She said she was just going to get water. Superego said.

Do you really believe that? Or was it an excuse to get away and notify someone? Id raised an eyebrow.

Jeanette wouldn't lie to us. Superego refused to entertain the possibility.

Yeah. Everyone is so wonderful and caring around here… Id rolled her eyes.

The longer Jeanette was away, the more my entrails nagged. Something was wrong, and I couldn't put my finger on it. Why was it taking her so long to get water?

After 20 long and agonizing minutes, Mom walked through the door. Part of me froze, knowing what prompted her guest appearance. Part of me was genuinely shocked, having not expected her.

"Hey babe." Mom half smiled at me.

"Hi." I mumbled. I waited for her to make the first move, unsure of what the future held.

"What's say we go home?" She extended her hand, offering to help me out of the chair.

"Why?" I furrowed my eyebrows at her.

"Come on. We have a lot to talk about." Helping me up, Mom wrapped her arms around me, walking me to the car.

Son of a bitch! I told you it was bad! Id screamed.

Now, now. Maybe they're trying to help. You don't know what's going on. Superego countered.

The hell I don't know! There's one way to fix things, and that's their way! It doesn't matter if the circumstances are different, or if the child is different! The only way to get things done is the adults' way! We are so screwed! Id shook her head, biting her lip.

We rode the rest of the ride home in silence. I really wanted mom to open the conversational door so that I could follow her through it, but it didn't seem like she was quite willing to do so.

I had so many questions I wanted to ask her. What was going to happen now? Why did she come pick me up from school? What did

Jeanette say to her? Did Jeanette even call her? How many other people know? What does everyone think about what I said?

When we pulled into the driveway, I was overcome with relief at the thought of escaping to my computer. Sitting at my computer, I would be alone. I wouldn't have to worry about anyone, or what they thought, or said, or did, or anything.

Every nanosecond was an hour's delay as I yearned for my computer, and I bounded like a puppy up the stairs, eagerly rushing to my best friend.

November 5, 2006 10:53am

Today is not looking good. I got called down to the guidance department, and I think I said something that freaked other people out. I didn't mean to. I wish I could take it back. I just want to be left alone, but I have a feeling they're going to be up my ass even more now. Why can't they just leave me alone? That's all I want. I don't bother them. Why do they bother me? Well, I'm going to take a nap. I don't want to deal with this shit right now.

Chapter 17

Leaning my head to the left with my hand on the right side of my neck, I strained against the ligaments until I heard a crack. I let out a small breath as I pushed against my knuckles. They sounded like packing bubbles as they popped. As I braced my legs around the computer chair in anticipation of cracking my back, I heard a light tap at the door.

"Come in." I called, pulling myself around until my spine sounded like a set of firecrackers going off.

"Don't do that! You could hurt yourself!" Mom scolded, wincing at the sounds.

"What's up?" I asked, ignoring her comments.

"I just wanted to talk." Mom sat on my bed.

You couldn't talk to me the entire car ride home, and now you want to talk? I thought bitterly. I hated when people did something after they squandered the opportunity to do it. That drove me nuts!

"Okay." I said, spinning the chair around so I could face her. "What's up?"

"I was going to ask you that." Leaning back, she crossed her right leg over her left one.

"Okay… Nothing…" I stared at mom unblinking, indicating that I was in the dark.

"That's not what Miss Benton said." Her tone was condescending.

"Okay." As more words floated out of Mom's mouth, the less interested I was in hearing the next one come out.

"She says that you have deep rooted anger issues." She shifted her legs.

I sat there, not saying a word. As far as I was concerned, this conversation was already over. I had tried previously on numerous occasions to explain to the adults how I felt, and no one wanted to listen then. This time was no exception.

"Hello? I'm talking to you." Mom pushed her head forward, emphasizing her words.

"I'm listening," I snipped. My lower jaw clenched as my eyes blurred from the anger welling up from deep inside my soul.

"Is that the case?" She snipped back.

"Is what the case?" I repeated.

"Do you have anger issues?" Mom folded her arms.

"I don't know. Do I?" I asked, folding my own arms.

"Robin Rachael, do you have to be so difficult? I'm trying to help you, but I can't do that if I don't know what's going on. So tell me what the heck is going on!" She threw her hands up in the air, exasperated.

"I don't know!" I snapped.

"How about you tell me what you do know?" Mom asked, folding her arms again.

"I know everybody sucks." I sneered.

"I swear…" Mom sighed.

"What?!" My breath escaped quickly. My mind started to race with words and ideas as I frantically tried to grasp the right one, the one that if I handed it to Mom, she would go away.

"I'm trying to help you! Why are you making everything so difficult?" Her shoulder slumped in partial defeat.

"I'm not trying to make everything so difficult." My heart twinged with guilt.

"I'm going to go take a bath." She stood up and walked towards the door. As her hand wrapped around the knob, she turned to look at me.

144

"You might want to figure out what's going on soon, because we have a meeting at the school tomorrow." With that, she left.

"What?!" I shrieked, chasing after her. "What meeting?"

"You, me, Mr. Mitchell, and Mr. Petersen are going to sit down and figure out what's the best thing to do with you. Mr. Mitchell doesn't want you around the other students if you're a problem." Mom closed the bathroom door.

"If I'm a problem?!" I asked incredulously, running back to my room and throwing myself on my bed. My eyes bulged out of their sockets. Did I hear her right?

"I didn't mean to upset you." Mom called softly from my bedroom door.

I could feel hot tears of anger threatening to erupt as my fists shook, pleading to release their wrath.

"Talk to me, honey. I don't like seeing you like this." She came and sat on the bed, trying to console me. "What can I do to help?"

"I'm the fucking problem?!" I shrieked from the pillow. My anger was feening for steam as I reiterated the question.

"The administration seems to think so." Mom slowly nodded.

Cute. That's really fucking cute. Id gritted her teeth.

I don't think you're bad. A smirk slowly crept over her left cheek, its shadow illuminating her dimple.

I chose to focus on my breathing instead of searching for the right words to say. My breath was hot and wet as it bounced off the pillow back into my face.

"Talk to me, babe. Tell me what you're feeling." Mom rubbed my back.

"It's not going to help." I sighed, taking in a deep breath.

"It might make you feel better. Seriously, tell me what you're feeling. Just let it out." She urged.

"I'm pissed off!" I shrieked.

"Why? What's making you mad?"

"I haven't done anything bad. How can they sit there and call me bad when I haven't done anything?!"

"Nobody's calling you bad honey. They're just worried about a comment you made to a lady in the guidance department." To no avail, Mom continued to rub my back in an effort to calm me down.

"What comment?" I snipped, although deep in my heart I knew what Mom was referring to.

"Miss Benton thinks you're going to hurt other students because you asked how they would feel if you did it to them."

I paused, trying to think of what to say. I knew if I had any hope of being understood (fully or in partial) by anyone, it would be my mother who could understand what I was trying to say. If only I could find the words…

"Well?" Mom asked, waiting for a response.

"Well what? How would they feel if they were being bullied? They wouldn't like it." I spat, sticking by my words. I was buying time, trying to articulate the true meaning.

"Are you saying you want to hurt them?" She squinted her eyes at me as her brows gracefully slid down her face.

"No, mom. I wouldn't hurt anyone. I'm just saying…" I sighed again.

"I think I know what you're trying to say." Mom nodded. "I think what you're trying to say is that when they pick on you, it hurts, and you don't think they'd like to feel that way. Is that correct?"

"Kind of, but they're not just picking on me. They're also kicking the crap out of me! And I don't do it to them! How would they like it if it happened to them?" I sniffled.

"So why are you really mad?" Mom asked.

"I'm mad because they're accusing me of shit that I don't do and that I would never do!" I fumed.

"Honey, please watch your language." She sighed.

"Sorry mom. I'm just so mad…" I let my voice trail off.

"I understand, and I think you're doing a great job of communicating. Lately, it's been hard to talk to you, but you're doing a great job right now. What else is going on?" Mom pried.

"Like what?" I asked, confused.

"Everything. I want to know everything so that I can help fix things. The more I know, the more I can help you." She smiled at me as I peeked an eye out from within the pillow.

"I just want to be left alone. I don't bother anyone, and they need to stop bothering me. I don't want to go talk to the guidance department. I don't want to work with other kids on projects. I don't want to see Mr. Mitchell about every little stupid thing. I just want to be left alone." My heart broke at the thought of the unfulfilled desire of solitude.

"Okay. Why do you want to be left alone?"

"I just do. I'm not bothering anyone, so why do they have to bother me?"

"You're saying you want them to stop being mean to you." Mom corrected.

"No, I want to be left alone." I corrected mom.

"What if they're trying to be nice to you?" She asked.

"Yeah, because that's ever going to happen." I rolled my eyes.

"You can't shut everyone out." Mom scolded.

"I don't. I just want to be left alone."

"Okay, moving on. Talk to me about this cell phone thing." Mom tried her hand of luck on a new topic.

"It's crap."

"Why? What makes it 'crap', as you call it?" Mom asked.

"Mr. Mitchell told me he wanted me to call you when there was a problem instead of leaving. I go to call you during lunch, and I get detention. If I had just left and not called you, I would've got detention." I rolled my eyes again.

"What about going to Mr. Mitchell and discussing the problem with him?"

"Yeah, that's a great idea. Run to Mr. Mitchell when someone's giving me problems, and then someone else will give me crap when their friend gets in trouble." I sneered.

"He's just trying to help." Mom offered.

"Yeah. Trying." I rolled my eyes.

"What would you do if you were in his position?" Mom asked.

"Huh?" Her question caught me off guard.

"What would you do if you were Mr. Mitchell?" She repeated.

My whole being grinded to a halt. It was as if my mind's fingers were covered in the slick slimy ignorance of youth, unable to tangibly perceive the simple concept that Mom was trying to portray to me.

"Uhhh…" I stammered.

"That's what I thought." A smug smile graced her lips. "How can you complain about his solution when you can't come up with one of your own?"

"I didn't say I couldn't come up with one on my own. I'm just saying, I wouldn't keep doing what he's doing." I spat, pouting like a child desperate to succeed in a failing argument.

"And what is Mr. Mitchell doing wrong?" Mom asked.

"Well, he keeps talking to the other kids. That's not doing anything, because they keep giving me crap. Talking isn't making it stop." I said slowly.

"Okay… What else?" Mom urged me to continue.

"I don't know. I don't know why they beat me up and give me crap every day. I wish I knew. I also wish I knew how to make it stop." I sighed and closed my eyes, trying to dissolve in the moment.

"Why do you think they pick on you?" She tilted her head at me in curiosity.

"Because they suck." I snickered.

"Seriously. Why." Mom asked, crossing her arms.

"I don't know why." I shrugged, opening my eyes wide in innocent ignorance.

"Well, the leading theory is that people bully other people because they're not happy with themselves, and it makes them feel better about themselves. What do you think about that?" Mom asked.

"I don't like it." I shook my head.

"Why not?"

"Because everyone has to have something good going in their life. Why bully someone if not everything sucks?" I asked.

"What's good in your life?"

"Solitaire." I laughed.

"Robin Rachael…" Mom playfully smacked me. "Seriously. What's good in your life?"

"I don't know." I shrugged.

"Is everything that bad?" She asked.

"No, it's not. It just sucks at school."

"But everything's good at home?" She pressed.

"Yeah." I shrugged slightly.

"Okay, then why do you think people bully other people?"

"I don't know. Why do you keep asking me?" I furrowed my eyebrows in playful anger.

"I'm trying to figure out a solution. Don't you want a solution to this?" Mom furrowed her eyebrows back at me.

"Yes, I do. Why are you making that face at me?" I shook my furrowed brows at her.

"Why are you making that face at me?" Mom squealed, then cracked up in laughter.

I rolled my eyes at her. "You are such a goofball, mom!"

"You are such a goofball!" She rolled her eyes back at me and pushed me gently. "So tell me then. If you don't think kids bully because they're not happy with themselves, then why do they bully?"

" Because they suck." I laughed.

"Robin…" Mom sighed, shaking her head. I could tell she was starting to get annoyed.

"No, I'm serious mom!" I stopped laughing.

"What do you mean by that?" A harsh sternness crept into her voice.

"Well, you said that kids bully because they're not happy with themselves, and it's a way to make themselves feel better. What if it doesn't make them feel better?" I asked.

"Then why would they do it?" She asked me.

" Because they suck!" I repeated. "Think about it. If they really think they're that bad, and someone else is worse, wouldn't it make them happy? Because then they're not that bad." I blinked.

"I think I understand what you mean. Kids don't just bully each other because it makes them feel better. Bullying allows them to focus on other people's problems rather than their own." Mom nailed my inners thoughts on the head!

"Yeah!" For the first time, it felt like someone was actually listening and working with me on a true solution!

"Okay. I gotcha. How about you answer my original question."

"Which was?"

"If you were Mr. Mitchell, what would you do to fix this problem?" Mom reiterated.

"I don't know." I shook my head, feeling my heart tear from the gravity of her question.

"So tell me what you do know." Mom reiterated.

"I know that they enjoy doing it. They laugh at me when they bully me. And I know talking to them and giving them detention doesn't work, because they do it again and again and again." I sighed.

"Do you think the punishment isn't severe enough?" Mom asked thoughtfully.

"No I don't." I shook my head again.

"Then what kind of punishment would you hand down to students caught bullying another student?" Mom asked.

"Me personally?"

"Yes you."

"I would first hold a meeting and find out the entire story, instead of listening to one side of it." I began, thinking bitterly about the detention Mr. Mitchell assigned me that stemmed from the cell phone incident.

"Okay. Then what?" Mom urged me to continue.

"If someone is bullying someone, then give them out of school detention for a week. And they have to go out on the highway and clean the sides of the roads!" I smiled.

"You mean community service?" Mom asked incredulously, her hand flying up to her mouth.

"Yeah." My grin was wide enough to let me swallow a 20 lb roast whole.

"That's a little extreme, don't you think?"

"No. They should be too scared to do it again."

"So you think that if the punishment were severe, that it would be a good deterrent?" Mom pondered my words.

"Yup." I nodded fervently as the vindictive ire in my soul caressed me.

Mom's hand rubbed her mouth, trying to stimulate the muscles into formulating a response. Blinking, she just stared at me.

"Let's take this one step at a time." Mom said slowly, still rubbing her mouth. "You mentioned having a meeting, right?"

"Yeah."

"What's the purpose of the meeting?" Mom asked.

"To find out what really happened." My forehead crinkled in confusion. I thought the answer was obvious, and yet she asked the question anyways.

"So the meeting is a quest for the truth." Mom ventured slowly into the mind of her adolescent daughter, searching to meet me in some kind of a middle ground that wasn't murky.

"Yeah." I nodded.

"I would think that the meeting wouldn't be the best idea." Mom furrowed her brows, bringing some adult experience to the tundra of teenage wisdom.

"Why not?"

"One of the parties might lie. For example, that one girl in the hall way claimed that you were antagonizing her, trying to get her to fight with you. What do you propose to do in that case?" Mom asked.

"I don't know. I guess the liar will be told to tell the truth." I shrugged.

"How can you tell when someone's lying?" Mom kept bombarding me with questions.

"I don't know! That's Mr. Mitchell's job, not mine." I snapped. I hated being pushed, regardless of the scenario. If I didn't know something, I didn't know something. Quit badgering me to 'know' something that I didn't!

Calm down, honey. She's trying to work with you, not fight you. Don't get yourself all worked up. Just take a breath, think rationally, and try to work out a solution with her. Superego whispered.

Fuck that! Just nod like everything's okay, then blast those sons of bitches! Guarantee that when we get to that stupid meeting, nobody else is going to listen to you! And then what? Shit's going to go back to normal. Everyone's going to kick your ass, and you're going to get more bullshit for them giving you shit. Id rolled her eyes.

Don't say that. Give them a chance. Superego scolded.

How many chances do they need? Id sneered.

I took a deep breath. I knew my inner feelings were right, but there was another feeling that was buried further than either one of them could reach. I couldn't quite put my finger on it, though.

"Okay, well that is a good idea. What else do you think needs to be done to handle bullying?" Mom asked, treading in a new direction.

"I still think that if someone bullies someone, that they should be expelled." I looked her right in the eye.

"I wouldn't go so far as to enforce a 'zero tolerance' policy, but I do agree that stricter punishments need to be handed out. Do you think that it was fair for the cheerleader to go to jail?"

"Yes and no." I shrugged.

"Why yes and why no?" Her hand began to pet my hair, trying to straighten the tangled mess that had accrued.

"Jail sucks, but she did break the law. Besides, I don't think she ever saw how bad my eye looked." My fingertips gingerly went to the still tender cut above my eye socket. I wondered what the discoloration of the bruising had morphed into.

"Did you want her to see how bad it was?" Mom asked.

"Yeah! It was nasty!" I shrieked, a smile pursing my lips.

"I think that's a good idea." Mom nodded.

"What?" The smile faded as confusion took over.

"I think she should've seen how bad your eye looked. To my knowledge, very few bullies are forced to face the aftermath of their abuse." I could see the gears in Mom's brain moving, although I had no idea which thoughts were fueling their movement.

"Bet she wouldn't have liked it if it were her eye." I mumbled.

"Robin! That's a great idea!" Mom jumped with excitement, her face animated by a passionate epiphany.

"What?!" I cried, my gut instinct telling me to retreat.

"Not only do very few bullies face what they've done, but I'm willing to bet they have no idea what their behavior feels like to the person on the receiving end!" Delight lit Mom's entire face up like the wintry holiday season.

"True." I nodded.

"What if we incorporated that into the meeting? Kind of like a backwards role-playing scenario?" Mom smiled at me.

"I think that's a good idea, but I do think that they need a more severe punishment. I mean, seriously. If they just get detention, what's the incentive to stop?" I broached the subject again, seeking approval.

"I agree with you, but I don't think community service is the answer. Why do you want them to do highway clean up?" Mom asked, wrinkling her forehead at me.

" Because everyone driving by will stare at them, and they'll get embarrassed!" I grinned.

"So you think public humiliation would be a better deterrent than just assigning detention?"

"Yep." I continued to nod in agreement.

"What if the bully had to make a public apology to their victim?" Mom asked. That's mom for you. Always trying to find the nicest solution.

"You mean in front of everybody?" My own gears tried to move, frantically grasping the concept she threw at me.

"Yes." She nodded.

"I guess, at long as it embarrasses them." I shrugged.

"Why do you want them to be publicly humiliated?" Mom shook her head.

" Because I know that when everyone's staring at me when I've done something wrong, I don't want to do it again. I don't want to be stared at. It's awful!" My cheeks burned at the recently acquired memory of when I was late to English, and everyone watched me take my seat.

"That's a good point. How about we discuss these points in the meeting tomorrow, and call it a day for now?" Mom stood up, getting ready to leave.

"Okay." I stood up and stretched, mentally bracing myself for my impending rendezvous with my technological friend.

November 5, 2006 12:01 pm

Well, mom and I talked for quite a bit today. She was mad earlier that I left school, but oh well. I'm sick of Mr. Mitchell giving me crap! I'm not a bad kid, and he needs to worry about the kids who are bad! But I guess we have a meeting tomorrow. Mom's going to mention a couple of things we talked about in there. Hopefully, Mr. Mitchell listens. He's such an asshole! Alright, I'm going to take a nap.

Chapter 18

As I lay in bed in a lucid state of unconsciousness, I was vaguely aware of the impending doom that was to become my judgment day. Regardless of what my own feelings were surrounding high school and everyone involved, I was now thought of as the "black sheep", destined to wreak havoc on all.

What you need to do is tell them how you feel. Superego said. *You need to explain to them you're not a bad kid and that you resent the implications.*

Fuck that! What you need to do is beat their asses and tell them to get out of your face! Tell them that you will leave them alone and they'd better leave you alone! Id retorted.

There's no need to resort to violence. She is more than intellectually capable of explaining how she feels using words. Superego rolled her eyes.

I was torn between their two worlds when a door slamming snapped me back into reality. I had been so out of it that I was unaware of anyone coming or going.

Curiosity seductively beckoned me with its hands, suggesting I investigate. No sooner had I sat up in bed then I began to hear unfamiliar clacking noises emanating from the kitchen.

What the hell is that? I thought, puzzled. *What is that rapid click click click coming from*?

In stealth mode I crept down the stairs, hoping to arrive undetected. Despite my best attempts, I had failed.

"Oh, hey you. Sorry I left. I had to go pick up something at work." Mom said with a faint smile.

"What's that noise I heard?" My eyebrows furrowed in confusion.

"What noise?" Mom asked.

"That clicking noise." I said.

"Oh. It was probably him." Mom pointed to a small, uncertain, black ball of fur on the floor.

"What is it?" I leaned to the left, trying to get a clearer view of this foreign entity.

"For your information, it is a dog, not an It." Mom spoke sternly.

"Why is there a dog in the house?" Now I was really confused.

"Because this guy I work with abused him, so I took him." Mom sat down on the stool at the island.

"What?! Why?" I was shocked. This fur ball couldn't have been more than 5 or 6 lbs, and he was maybe the size of my shoe. He was so fragile. How could anyone have hurt him?

"Well, this guy I work with owned him and would come into work bragging about kicking him and throwing him. He said he would treat the dog like that because every time he went near the dog, the dog would nip at him. Well, what do you expect when you mistreat a poor little thing like that? You can't beat him and hurt him and expect him to be happy and cuddle up to you. Anyways, he said he was going to kill the dog, so I took him." Mom shrugged.

Gee, you can understand why a dog would react violently when it's mistreated, but you can't understand why she gets upset when everyone at school treats her like crap? Id sneered.

Stop that. How is anyone supposed to know what she's feeling if she doesn't communicate it? Superego sighed.

Easy. Who likes getting in trouble all the time, having the other kids pick on her, and everyone tells her she's a bad kid? Nobody, that's who. Id rolled her eyes.

I took a mini step towards him, and he crouched on the floor. What I presumed was his tail slightly thumped against the floor as he peered up at me. He had such large eyes for being so small!

"Hi, little guy." I said softly, reaching my hand out. I squatted down so that he was able to sniff me.

"His name is Shadow. And don't get too attached. He's only staying here until I find a good home for him." Mom said.

"Hi Shadow." My hand was less than an inch in front of his nose, and he curiously sniffed it. I smiled at his loving nature, and gently pet the top of his head. He ran in between my legs and rested his front paws on my thigh.

"Awww, aren't you cute?" I laughed. His tail was thumping wildly as he regaled in delight.

But his eyes betrayed him. They looked heartbroken as they told a story of pain, rejection, and abuse. My own heart twinged with pain as our souls recognized the other's journey. We knew exactly how the other one felt, being an outcast, and wondering what you had done that was so bad to deserve being treated the way we were.

"Don't worry, buddy. I got you." I cooed, scooping him up in my arms as he began to lick my face furiously. It was funny to watch, because his tongue stuck out the left side of his mouth.

"Looks like you made a friend." Mom smiled.

"Looks like." I smiled back. As I cradled him in my arms, everything else faded off into the background. In that instant, I no longer cared about the meeting, or what everyone thought about me, or how they treated me. All I cared about was this sweet angel sent down to me from the heavens. He didn't care that everyone else gave me a hard time. He didn't care that they thought I was a bad person. To him, I was the answer to his prayers. I was a loving savior brought into his life to protect him.

"Don't get too attached." Mom echoed. "He's not staying forever."

But it was already too late.

■■

Dinnertime was fun. Mom and I sat down to eat on the couch, and Shadow was sweetly perched next to my feet.

"Can I help you?" I asked, smiling at him.

He wagged his tail, causing his little body to slightly shake with it.

"You are so cute!" I laughed.

His tail wagged furiously as he tried to climb up my legs and into my lap.

"He just wants your food." Mom smiled.

"I know. Can I give him some?" I turned my head to the left and looked at her.

"A little bit." She nodded slowly. "Give him a carrot."

Delicately I extended a piece to the newest addition, and he gobbled it up. I pulled my fingers back as terror slightly spiked at the prospect of being nibbled on myself.

"You're such a goober!" Mom laughed.

I just looked at her incredulously. "Well, excuse me!"

Looking back at the sweet face staring at me, he wagged his tail for more.

■■■I

The next morning, I was nervous. I wasn't in the mood to deal with everyone at school accusing me of heresy. They weren't going to stop with their witch hunt, and I wasn't going to stop for my quest in peace and solitude. We were on a one way track towards collision. The only question was: Who was going to come out slightly less battered?

As the car lurched forward, my mind kept flittering from topic to topic. Who all was going to be there? Was anyone going to defend me? Were they even going to listen to me? What was their argument going to be?

I tried to brace myself for the onslaught of accusations when Shadow's sweet face crept to the forefront of my mind. I couldn't help but smile at the thought of his loving innocence, his tail wagging. He didn't care what happened to me throughout my day. All he cared about was that I was nice to him, and in return, he was nice to me.

"Ready, babe?" Mom's voice retrieved me from the swirling clouds of chaos in my mind.

"Yeah, I guess." I sighed, slowly climbing out of the car.

"Aww, come on. It's not that bad." She rubbed my back.

"Yeah." The word facetiously darted out of my mouth as I looked up at her.

"Hey, I'm here with you. Don't worry." Mom smiled.

Those words jump started the anticipatory button in my brain, causing me to shake with fear. "Don't worry." Those were condescending words of doom, meant to soften the blow of any impending destruction.

As we walked towards the school, it took on an eerie and unfamiliarly menacing loom to it. I looked for any vestige of normalcy, but it was futile. Every step made my heart pound harder, and I instinctively reached for my mother's hand for protection.

"Aw, honey. Don't be scared." Mom could feel my hand shake inside hers, and she tried to give a reassuring squeeze. We turned into the main office, and I could see Mr. Mitchell and Mr. Petersen standing there talking amongst themselves. They seemed to be enjoying the mindless banter between them. I doubted they noticed we had arrived.

"Good morning, gentlemen." Mom smiled as she walked over to them.

"Good morning, Annie." They greeted her in unison.

"Shall we get started?" Mr. Mitchell waved in the direction of his office.

The adults mumbled some kind of agreement as I tagged along behind them. Once again, I was merely a spectator and not a participant. I chose to sit in the chair in the corner while the adults hovered around his desk.

"To what do I owe the pleasure of this meeting?" Mr. Petersen smiled at mom.

"Well, lately Robin has felt like there have been a lot more problems at school." Mom began.

"What kind of problems?" The males echoed.

Right. Like you honestly care. Id rolled her eyes.

They wouldn't be asking if they didn't. Superego said.

Bullshit! People never say what they mean or mean what they say. They're just asking what the problem is so that they don't look like total jerks! Id snipped.

Then why would they waste their time trying to help if they didn't mean it? Superego tilted her head thoughtfully to the left.

Wow. You are seriously dumb. You don't get it, do you? Id sneered.

Get what? Superego gritted her teeth.

THEY are the problems! Them and their ignorant mentality are the problems! Id yelled.

How are they ignorant? How are they the problem? Superego shook her head in confusion.

You cannot use double edged swords when dealing with issues. You can't tell someone 'do it this way' then punish them when they do. Id sighed in exasperation.

What are you talking about?! Now, her eyebrows furrowed in confusion.

'Oh, don't use your cell phone during your classes. What? You used it during your own time? Detention!' Id mocked.

That's not what happened and you know it! Superego yelped.

Oh, okay. Then what did? Id glared.

Mr. Mitchell asked if she could use the main office phone in case of a problem. That's all. There's nothing unreasonable about his request. Superego glared back.

Then why did he tell Mom is was okay if she used her cell phone to call for help, just as long as she didn't just walk home during the school day? Id countered.

You are so difficult. Superego sighed.

Their mindless chatter continued as ire filled me to the brim. I looked from face to face, and it was apparent that I blended in with the décor.

Why the hell was I even here? They were completely ignoring me! How did anyone expect to 'fix' anything if they didn't even know what the problem was?!

See? My girl kind of gets the drift. Id nodded.

No she doesn't. You've just corrupted her with your emotional tantrums! Superego snapped.

Yeah, okay. Maybe she sees my logic and you don't! Id stuck her tongue out.

What logic?! All you are doing is breaking the rules and whining about how everyone is picking on her! God! You seriously don't get it! Superego shook her head again.

What don't I get? Id crossed her proverbial arms against her proverbial chest.

There are rules in place for a reason. The reason is to keep everything running smoothly and keep everyone safe. If one too many people deviate from those rules, you'd have complete anarchy! Superego explained.

And you don't get it. Id sighed.

Fine. Explain it to me.

There may be rules in place, but this isn't 'one size fits all.' Everyone is different. How does that saying go? 'If everyone were the same, the world would be a boring place.' Well, if someone is giving her shit, and going to the adults don't help, then she has every right to leave. She's not fighting back. How fair is that? And she's the one who's getting in trouble for those bitches harassing her! Id rolled her eyes.

No one ever said that life was 'one size fits all.' They're just saying that you just can't do whatever you want! Superego seethed with anger.

Then what would you have her do, Ms. Know It All? Id rolled her eyes.

I think she's more than capable of expressing any issues and working <u>with</u> the administration to rectify any situation. Superego nodded.

And what about the issues they cause? Who the hell is she going to run to for help when they're the problem? Id countered.

I don't know. What do you propose to do that's reasonable? Id sighed.

Why does she have to comply with rules that don't make sense? I'm not saying she doesn't follow any rules. I'm just saying that if she is of a different character, then she should follow different rules.

Would you have everyone following different rules? Superego snapped.

No. Our girl is a good girl. She doesn't cause trouble. I think people should be a little bit more lenient on her. I think the students who are giving her a hard time should receive more discipline. Maybe even public humiliation... Id began.

How could you even suggest to embarrass an adolescent?! They're going through a hard enough time in their life as it is! Superego gasped.

And if it will deter them from being shit heads, then I say do it. No mercy. Id grinned.

Their banter was almost as bad as the one the adults were carrying on.

I decided to flip through my day, and figure out all of my options. I began with what I was going to do when this meeting was over. What was the resolution going to be? Was I going to any of my classes, or was I going to go home?

When I thought about home, an angelic image flashed before my eyes, and I couldn't help but smile. Those eyes pulled at my heartstrings every time. Regardless if I wanted to have a heart of ice and lock everyone out, he alone had the power to melt it.

"Robin? Are you there?" Mom's hand waved in front of my face, and I blinked.

"Huh?" Looking around, I could see all eyes on me.

"Mr. Petersen asked you a question." Mom said.

"Oh. Sorry." I looked at the floor as a pain twinged my heart. They had intentions of involving me in their discussion, and I had immediately dismissed them as ignorant adults.

"I asked you what you thought was going on." Mr. Petersen smiled at me.

I shrugged. "I don't know."

"Oh, come on. You can talk to me. No one is going to give you trouble." He placed his hand on my shoulder, offering his reassurance.

"I think its crap." I looked into his kind face as he studied mine.

"Robin! Watch your language!" Mom gasped.

"It's alright, Annie. Let her speak." He shushed mom. "What's crap?"

"Everything." I shrugged again.

"Like what? I'm trying to help, but I need to understand it from your point of view."

"I don't know. It's hard to explain." I shrugged. I knew in my heart what I wanted to say, but my head was unable to translate the internal messages.

"Okay. Where would you like to start?" Mr. Petersen asked.

"What about the incident with the cell phone that happened yesterday?" Mom offered.

"Why don't you tell me about it?" He smiled at me again.

I looked at Mr. Mitchell as he sat motionless. I knew to recount my version of what happened would put him and me at further odds, and I didn't know if that would trigger more trips to his office.

"Well, Mom gave me a cell phone to use in case something happened at school. So I tried calling her, and I got detention. But I tried calling her during my lunch! I didn't bother anyone by using it in class!" My hands flew up out of my lap, throwing my exasperation at the adults.

"And you got detention for using your cell phone during school hours?" Mr. Petersen asked.

"Yes. It's crap! Mom gave me a cell phone so I could call her because she didn't like me walking away." I snipped.

"Walking away from what?"

"Everything. The other students threaten me, and I leave rather than stay and get my butt kicked. Mr. Mitchell asked me to use a phone instead of just leaving. So I go to call my mom, and I get detention!" I spat.

"Why don't you come to me for help? If someone is giving you trouble, I'd like to know so that I can help you." Mr. Mitchell spoke softly.

I sighed, shaking my head.

"Well, I think it's a reasonable request. What's wrong with that?" Mr. Petersen furrowed his brows.

"Because."

"Because why?"

"Because it doesn't work like that." I said.

"How does it work then?" He rubbed my shoulder some more, trying to encourage me to open up.

"Because they're not going to stop. When the cheerleader hit me and got in trouble, one of her friends put rat poison in my locker! When she got in trouble, this kid Justin in my gym class threatened me." I whined.

My head began to throb as this logic train went faster and faster on its circular track.

"So what you're saying is that there will always be someone who is bullying you, and when something is done about one student, another student fills their void." Mr. Petersen stated.

"Yeah." I sighed sadly.

"Do you antagonize them?" He asked.

"No!" I jumped in my chair as Mr. Petersen quickly retrieved his hand.

"No, Robin's a good girl. She doesn't cause trouble. That's why all of these problems are so out of character for her. Something's wrong." Mom leaned in and gave me a hug.

"So what would you like the solution to be?" Mr. Petersen asked, leaning in. It would seem that the adults were flocking around me and not Mr. Mitchell. That made me smile on the inside.

"I don't know. I just want to be left alone. I don't bother anybody, and I don't want anyone to bother me. I come to school, I do my work, and I go home. I don't talk to anyone, I don't pick fights with anybody, nothing." I whined again.

"In a school with over 5,000 students, how are we going to isolate you?" Mr. Mitchell asked. His tone was low, so it was nearly impossible to tell if he was using his monotone or if he was upset.

"I don't know." I shrugged.

"You just want to be left alone." Mr. Petersen nodded.

"Well, the guidance counselor is afraid that you're going to hurt someone." Mom's statement resonated with concern.

"No mom." I rolled my eyes.

"Then what did you mean by what you said to her?" Mr. Petersen asked.

"I'm just saying, how would they like it if someone hurt them? How would they like it if someone treated them the way they treated me? I'm sure they'd be pretty upset." I snipped.

"If she's threatening the other students, maybe we should transfer her to an alternative school." Mr. Mitchell offered.

"What? Why?" Mom gritted her teeth and glared at him.

"Safety is our top priority at this school, along with obtaining a first rate education." Mr. Mitchell smiled hollowly.

"That's not fair. The other students open the door to violent behavior, and you want to persecute <u>my</u> daughter? I don't think so! Just because they're doing it to her does not give Robin permission to behave that way, and she knows that. But she's not the one who is instituting school violence! If you want to isolate the problems, I suggest you talk to the other students!" Mom spat.

"We have dealt with the other students appropriately, and we have taken extra precautions in order to ensure that the safety of our students is procured." Mr. Mitchell stated. "We have enlisted the help of the police as well as held several assemblies. The students know there is a zero tolerance policy in place, and that they will be dealt with severely and accordingly."

"Excuse me, Mr. Mitchell, but didn't a group of girls put rat poison in my daughter's locker after you had taken 'extra precautions'?" Mom retorted, folding her arms.

"I believe you are right, Annie." Mr. Petersen nodded.

"I am not trying to be condescending, Mr. Mitchell. I am merely pointing out that not enough has been done to stop bullying from occurring. These kids are able to hurt my daughter, and her education is beginning to suffer." Mom shot the principal a dagger look.

"I believe your daughter's education is beginning to suffer because she is cutting classes. She is taking matters into her own hands, rather than come to me for assistance." Mr. Mitchell shot back.

I sighed. This was why I couldn't go to Mr. Mitchell for help. He was a pompous ass who knew everything. Nobody was going to tell him he was wrong, wholly or impartially.

"Do you expect her to stay when people are threatening her?" Mom countered. I could tell Mr. Mitchell was beginning to get under her skin.

"As I mentioned, your daughter has not once come to me for help, so there's nothing I can do for her that I haven't already done."

I loved how they had begun to discuss me as if I wasn't here! I let my thoughts drift away to anywhere but here. I couldn't help but wonder what that angelic black ball of fuzz was doing in our absence.

"How can my daughter come to you for help when there are repercussions from the other students if she does?" It seemed as if Mom was about to slap the smugness out of Mr. Mitchell's expression.

"Your daughter should let me worry about the repercussions. I can handle it, and I'm willing to help her if she comes to my office and asks for it." Mr. Mitchell repeated.

"You can't honestly think that you can prevent a bully from retaliating on my daughter after you chastise one of their friends!" Mom asked incredulously.

"So what do you recommend?" Mr. Petersen asked Mom.

"Well, I was talking to Robin last night, and we agreed that a lot of changes need to happen in order to deter the other students from bullying…"Mom began.

"And what kind of changes do you think should transpire, Robin?" Mr. Petersen turned to face me.

"Uh, well…" I stammered. I wasn't sure how to respond to an adult as an adult. It was going to take me a while to formulate the correct response.

"It's okay, babe. Tell them what we discussed last night." Mom urged.

"Well, I don't think giving them detention is reason enough to stop. I think something more has to be done if they're not going to want to bully other kids." I said slowly.

"Something more. Like what?" Mr. Petersen asked.

"Well, mom mentioned something of a reverse role play or something." I looked up at him, and he appeared to genuinely be listening.

"Mm hmm. And what would that accomplish?" He nodded slightly.

"Well, I don't bully anyone because I know how it feels. It sucks. Do they know it sucks?" I asked.

"So what you're saying is that a role reversal might allow the bullies to understand how the other side feels, and then they might not be so inclined to do it." Mr. Petersen stated.

"Yeah, but I think they should do it in front of everyone. Maybe if everyone was staring at them, they'd be too embarrassed to do it again." I continued, a smirk gracing my face. I felt like Mr. Petersen was listening. He was truly on my side.

"Like in a classroom, or an assembly. Okay." He continued to mull over my words.

"But you shouldn't give the kid who was picked on detention. That's not fair to them." I shot Mr. Mitchell a dirty glare.

"You're absolutely right about that." Mr. Petersen looked at me.

"But the students can't take matters into their own hands. They need to come to the main office and alert the faculty. It's our job to intervene and keep order." Mr. Mitchell interjected.

Fuck you, asshole! You are just causing problems! You are a control freak who is lashing out at my girl because she won't cater to your stupid rules! Id screeched.

Hey now. Mr. Mitchell is at least sitting down and trying to discuss matters with her. Give him credit for trying. Superego furrowed her brows.

Yeah, I'll give him credit. He'd be the biggest contributor to my girl flipping out! Id sneered.

You're impossible. Superego sighed.

"I agree. The students can't take matters into their own hands, but I think more should be done to handle the situations that arise. If harassment is continuing while the police are here, then we need to switch our tactics." Mr. Petersen spoke softly. Mr. Mitchell shot me a look of anger, and then turned to face Mr. Petersen.

"So what do you recommend that we do, sir?" Mr. Mitchell asked.

"Why don't we give this role playing idea a go? I don't see what we have to lose at this point." Mr. Petersen offered.

Mom and I smiled at each other. It may not have been a perfect solution, but it was a step in the right direction. It was change, for the better.

"However, we need to discuss a plan in the event one student witnesses bullying and wishes to report it. I think there should be some kind of secret support system set in place so that students can anonymously report bullying, without having to worry that they're next." Mr. Petersen winked at me. I smiled back.

"Absolutely. That's a fabulous idea." Mom nodded. "What do you think, honey?"

"Sounds awesome." A faint glimmer of hope could be detected on my cardiac monitor, if I had been wearing one.

"Are there any other matters to discuss?" Mr. Petersen asked.

"As a matter of fact, there is." Mom piped up. "Robin came home from school yesterday. She said that an incident happened at lunch."

Mr. Mitchell nodded. "I remember. Rita brought her to my office because she was caught using her cell phone during school hours."

I wanted to jump out of my seat and claw his face off! How dare he paint me as a delinquent! What an ass!

"Robin, how about you tell your side?" Mr. Petersen pursed his lips.

"Well, Mom had a meeting with you yesterday morning, and I just wanted to see how it went." I stammered. My heart boxed against my ribs, each thud shaking the foundation of my being harder than the first.

"But there is a strict no cell phone policy in place, young lady. If you needed to use the phone, you could've come to the main office. We can't have other students being distracted by you using your cell phone." Mr. Mitchell sternly spat.

"That's why I waited until lunch. I was standing alone at my locker. I wasn't bothering anyone." I protested.

"But honey, if there's a no cell phone policy, then that means no cell phones." Mom said.

Are you kidding me?! *Now you're against me*?! I thought, shaking my head.

"Why are you shaking your head?" Mr. Petersen asked.

"Mr. Mitchell told me to call mom if there was a problem. So mom got me a cell phone so that I could. Then I get in trouble for using the phone to call her! It's crap!" I whined.

"I agree. You can't expect her to come running to the office every time there's a problem. If the other students see her running to you for help, they'll ostracize her even more." Mr. Petersen nodded.

Ha! *Fuck you, you fat bastard*! Id grinned.

Stop that! *That's not lady like*! Superego scolded.

"So I don't have detention?" I batted my lashes, trying to disguise the hopeful smile that loomed beneath the surface.

"Not this time. But let's compromise on this topic. You can use your cell phone during lunch times and study halls, but you have to be in the main office so that you won't distract the other students. Does that work for everyone?" Mr. Petersen inquired.

"Yes." I smiled.

"Absolutely." Mom smiled.

"Yes, sir." Mr. Mitchell mumbled.

"Are there any more matters to discuss?" Mr. Petersen asked.

"Does this mean I don't have lunch detention for trying to call mom?" My eyes opened wide with hope.

"No, not this time. Just make sure in the future you use your cell phone in the main office, okay?" Mr. Petersen rubbed my head.

"Yes sir!" I smiled.

"You will still receive detention for missing your afternoon classes." Mr. Mitchell grumbled. It was obvious that he wasn't about to give up all of his authority.

"Is that true?" Mr. Petersen asked.

"Yes sir." I looked down, my high spirits dashed.

"Why did you miss your afternoon classes?"

I was at a loss for words. How was I going to explain that I was sick of Mr. Mitchell constantly giving me detention?

"Well?" He rubbed my arm, trying to coax the information out of me.

I glanced at Mr. Mitchell, and his glare chilled my bone marrow. Mr. Petersen caught our visual exchange.

"Would you two excuse us and let us have a moment in private?" Mr. Petersen said to Mom and Mr. Mitchell. I blinked. Did he really just dismiss the other adults?

"Sure." They agreed in unison, slowing making their way to the main office.

"Now, dear. Please tell me what upset you so much that you left without permission." Mr. Petersen smiled at me.

"I don't know. It just seems like every single day, Mr. Mitchell is yelling at me and giving me detention. He told me that I had to call mom if there was a problem, then I get detention for calling mom! It doesn't seem fair!" I protested. "I'm not trying to cut classes…"

"It's just a lot to deal with." Mr. Petersen finished. "Tell me. How would you prefer your high school experience to be?"

"Um, quiet. I don't really talk to anyone." I shrugged.

"And you'd like it if they didn't bother you?" He asked.

"Yeah. I just want to do my work and go home."

"You won't have detention this time, but if anyone, including Mr. Mitchell, is upsetting you on a daily basis, you need to come to me. But for now, try to work with him on resolving problems. How does that sound?"

"Okay." I looked up at the compassion that radiated from his eyes.

"I don't want these four years to be difficult for you. I'd like you to thrive through them, not survive. Do you understand?"

"Yes sir." I nodded.

"You know, not every grown up is awful. Just don't tell my daughter that." He winked at me.

"You have a daughter?" My eyebrows furrowed in surprise.

"I do. She goes to a different school, though. She's only a year older than you, so I know how hard high school can be for a young lady." He smiled. I smiled back. I had an ally in my corner.

"Is there anything else?" He asked.

"No sir." I smiled.

"Okay then. Tomorrow, we will hold an assembly first thing in the morning that will announce the role playing idea. I will spend the rest of the day drawing up the blue prints for how this will transpire. If there's nothing else, than let's go meet up with your mom." Mr. Petersen stood up.

I leapt out of my seat, and follow his heels out the door. Rushing past him, I ran into mom.

"Did you two have a nice talk?" Mom asked.

"Yeah. He said that I can't be skipping classes, but I don't have detention this time." I smiled, shooting a smug look at Mr. Mitchell.

"And why is that?" Mr. Mitchell snipped.

"Because I can call Mr. Petersen if things are that bad." I smirked.

"But she should try to resolve the issues with you first." Mr. Petersen corrected. I didn't want to say that because Mr. Mitchell was the kind of person who would push his way on everyone else, and I was the kind of person who wouldn't back down and put up with his crap.

"Okay." Mr. Mitchell stated. He wasn't happy that I wasn't going to receive detention, but he was going to have to live with the couple of inches he was left in control of.

"As I told Robin, I am going to draw up the details for the role playing and we will hold an assembly tomorrow morning in front of the entire study body. As for now, the meeting is adjourned." Mr. Petersen smiled.

"Thank you very much!" I smiled, hugging the superintendent.

"Come on, kiddo. I've got to get to work. Let's get going." Mom tugged on my hair gently.

"Okay." Letting go of Mr. Petersen, I flashed a huge grin as I skipped out of the office. Mom wasn't far behind.

"Where are we going?" I asked, bouncing around to face her.

"Well, I'm taking you home and then I'm going to work." She informed me.

"Why am I going home?" Immediately, I regretted my question. I didn't want to seem eager to go to school. I couldn't imagine anyone my age being excited! I knew that students like that existed, but the idea was ridiculous!

"I already called you out for today, unless you want to go to school." Mom grinned at me.

"No, that's okay." I laughed, shaking my head.

"That's what I thought."

Giddily, I scampered off towards the car. I was ecstatic at having a mini break. I didn't have to deal with the other students, and best of all, I didn't have to deal with Mr. Mitchell!

"Just make sure you take the dog out," Mom called from the car window.

"Okay!" I threw over my shoulder as I darted into the house. I ran as fast as I could to my computer.

November 6, 2006 11:13am

That was awesome! Mr. Petersen said I didn't have any detention! Haha!

Fuck you, Mr. Mitchell! He's such an asshole! And I guess Mr. Petersen is

going to try the role playing idea of mom's. I still think that bullies should

be publicly humiliated! Maybe they'd think twice about pulling that shit

again! Oh yeah! And mom brought home a dog yesterday! He's so cute!

But she said we can't keep him. I really hope we do. He's so cute and

sweet! Well, I'm going to go take the dog out and play with him. It's so

awesome! I have the rest of the day off! And I get to play with the puppy!

Chapter 19

I bounced down the stairs on an air of happiness. For the first time in a long time, I had no concerns. Making my way back to the entrance, I saw a small cat carrier on the floor.

"Hi, little guy." I cooed as I reached for the latch on the front.

A high pitched whine floated up to me, and I could see his petite frame shake wildly with excitement.

"Want to go outside?" I laughed at his enthusiasm as the front gate swung open. "Come on." Opening the glass sliding door, I exited and waited for him to follow. I didn't have to for long, because he was right on my heels.

"Go on. Go potty." I waved him towards the grass, and he just stared at me. Rolling my eyes at him, I sat down on the patio floor. He scooted up to me, crawling into my lap.

"No, no, no. Go potty." I laughed, gently placing him on the patio floor.

After a few minutes of me removing him, he got the hint and headed over to the grass. As he wandered around to find the perfect spot, the "What if?" monster snuck up on me.

What if this role playing idea doesn't pan out? We should have an alternate solution to this problem. Superego whispered.

We already have an alternate solution. Chlorine gas the entire school! Id grinned.

That's not reasonable! Superego spat.

You never said anything about reasonable. Id kept grinning.

Seriously. We should think about a better solution. I do like the role playing idea, but not everyone will be receptive to the idea. How are we going to handle bullying from now on? Superego questioned.

Easy. We pop them in their smug faces! Id laughed.

You are impossible! Robin, don't listen to her! Listen to me! Superego pleaded. *Things aren't hopeless! You are smart, beautiful, talented... You can find a better solution than stooping to violence!*

Oh sure, you could find 'a better solution,' or you could take a stand and let them know you won't put up with being everyone's punching bag. Id shrugged.

Do you know when heliocentrism was originally theorized? Superego asked.

What the hell does that have to do with anything? Id raised an eyebrow.

Humor me. Do you know? Superego repeated.

No. Id spat.

The first person to mention it was Aristarchus of Samos around 270 BC. Do you know when the church stop considering it heresy? Superego asked.

No. When? Id rolled her eyes.

Around 1822. Superego informed.

What does that have to do with anything? Id was getting annoyed with her logical counterpart.

My point is that sometimes change is gradual, that things we believe to be common sense is offensive to others. You expect the other students to

leave her alone because when they bully her, it hurts her. Do you think
they have the mental capacity to empathize with anyone? No, they don't.
They can barely see anything that doesn't revolve around themselves.

Id's mouth dropped. *Are you seriously bashing other people?*

No, I'm not. I'm just saying that between puberty and the development
of their frontal lobes, these 'tweens' are just beginning to mature into a
person that is separate from their parents. Being the first generation of
students who are expected to understand repercussions before they
happen and anticipate other people's feelings is a lot to ask if they've
never had to do it before. It doesn't make it impossible. It just means you
have to be patient while they learn how. Other generations will lead by
example. But that doesn't mean that this change is going to be easy.
Superego lectured.

Regardless if it's easy, these bastards need to learn that they're not the
only person on this planet! They're gonna be in for a surprise when they
go out into the real world and find out that no one gives a shit about them
and they're not as special as mommy and daddy tell them they are! Id
cackled.

You need to learn patience. Don't you know anything about human behavior? Superego shook her head.

I know plenty. I know that some people just don't get it, and they need a severe shock in order to get the hint. Id began punching her left palm.

True, but violence is not the way to teach people. Most people are resistant to the idea that something they're doing is bad. They believe that it makes them bad, and they have a hard time separating the idea of bad behavior and bad person. Besides, all violence teaches people is that it's okay to use it. And it's not.

I knew what my gut instinct was trying to tell me. That not everyone would be receptive to this radical new way of dealing with bullies. Most people would be resistant to change, at first. That doesn't mean that it wasn't necessary, or inevitable. But it wasn't going to be easy. And I knew that if anyone found out that it was my idea, I would catch way more shit than I was getting now.

Taking a deep breath, I could feel the weight of the "What if?" monster crushing my spirits. I could feel the tears begin to well up as my breath caught in my throat.

A light sensation tickled the top of my left hand, and I jumped back to reality. Jerking my head to the left, I saw the origin of the feathery touch. It was Shadow's paw. His giant eyes looked so sad and hopeful as he peered up at me.

"Aww. You want to hold my hand?" A huge smile graced my cheeks as I ran my fingers through his fur. His tail lashed the patio floor as he scooted up into my lap.

"Come on, buddy. Let's go upstairs." Delicately, I scooped him into my arms and carried him up the stairs. Placing him on my bed, I laid down on my side to face him.

His nose magnetized to mine as the slight sounds of rapid air flow blasted me in the face.

"Quit it!" I laughed, rubbing my nose. He panted, wagging his tail in delight.

I threw a blanket over him and asked, "Where'd you go? Where's Shadow?"

I could hear him whine as he raced in all directions, trying to find any escape. Laughing, I flipped over the blankets.

"There you are!" I grinned, and he pounced on my face to kiss me.

"Awww. I love you too, buddy." My hand slid down his back for several thousand strokes, and the "What if?" monster had all but faded to the back of my mind...

■■■

"Hello?" A voice called from the hallway.

"Hello, hello!" I responded, looking up from the puppy.

"Did you two have fun?" Mom's head appeared in the doorway.

"Yeah. He's so cute." I smiled.

"I'm glad you think so. Don't forget, he's not staying forever."

"I know. What's up?" I asked, desperate to change the subject. I didn't want to think about losing this sweet angel.

"Not much. Work was awful. My boss lost the spreadsheets I printed for him. And right in the middle of an audit!" Her hands went flying, trying to push away the frustration she'd built up throughout the day.

"I'm sorry." I pushed my lower lip out.

"It's not your fault, kiddo." She plopped on the bed, her hands wandering to her feet. Shadow perked up at the added weight, immediately jumping up to investigate.

"Oh, please don't!" I whined, bursting into laughter.

"Don't what?" She snipped, staring at me.

"Please don't take your shoes off!" It was getting harder to breathe as my diaphragm pulsated.

"You're so mean!" Mom playfully pushed me, and Shadow pounced on our point of contact.

"Rowr!" He squeaked.

"Awww. He doesn't like violence." As I steadied my weight with my right hand, my left hand went to stroke him.

"That's so weird. I didn't think animals reacted strongly against violence. I guess it's understandable, considering the abuse he went through." Mom stood up and stretched.

"Where are you going?" Desperate to change the subject, I threw out the first thing that came to mind. It still hit a nerve that she understood the resentment of abuse in an animal, but not from her own daughter.

"I thought I'd go relax. Why don't you come bug me in an hour, and we'll discuss dinner?" Mom kept walking out the door.

"Okay." I meandered over to my computer, my nerves beginning to get the better of me.

November 6, 2006 5:53 pm

I don't know why, but I'm getting nervous. I keep wondering about the assembly tomorrow. I wonder what's going to happen. I wonder how the other students are going to take it. Are they going to get mad at me? Are they going to know it was because of me? I hope not! I'm getting so sick of this shit! I had fun today though. It was nice to stay home and play with the dog. I know mom says we're not keeping him, but he's so cute! Earlier, we were playing hide and seek! He's such a silly puppy! When I throw a blanket on him, he goes nuts trying to find his way out! It's hilarious! Well, I'm going to go bug mom. She mentioned something about dinner. Plus, I want to know if we can keep the puppy!

Chapter 20

"Hey mom?" I peered into her room, doing a quick scan for signs of life.

"Yeah?" I could see her leaning into her closet. I wasn't sure what she was fetching.

"I was wondering if we could talk." I tiptoed over to her.

"Sure. What about?" She didn't even glance up at me.

"Tomorrow."

"What about tomorrow?"

"The assembly." I started rubbing my left thumbnail. It was a nervous habit I'd developed. I did it to distract myself.

"What about it honey? Are you nervous?" She finally leaned back out of the closet, her eyes softening at the corners as her corneas absorbed my emanating concern.

"Yeah."

"What about it concerns you? Come sit on the bed and talk to me." Mom took my hand, gently pulling me over to the bed.

"I'm just worried. I don't want the other kids to find out it was me and give me more crap." I sighed as I flopped onto her bed.

"Oh honey. I wouldn't worry about it so much." Mom rubbed my shoulder. "Would you like to hear a story?"

"Sure mom." I exhaled, pushing the listless words out.

"When I was in high school, the most popular girl always made fun of me. It didn't matter the reason. She made fun of me because I was skinnier than she was, because my hair was shorter than hers, yada yada. You get the picture. Any reason she could make fun of me, she did. She was very popular with the boys, and I preferred books."

"Well, long story short, the summer after we graduated, I was working as a cashier in a department store. Lo and behold, guess who walks in the door just before Christmas time! It was her! Except she wasn't alone. She was pushing a stroller with two babies in it, and she was pregnant with her third child. Can you imagine! Being 19 years old, having 2 babies and on her way to having a third! That poor thing." Mom shook her head.

Well, if she wasn't such a slut, she wouldn't have gotten herself into that mess. Id rolled her eyes.

Stop that! You should feel sorry for that poor girl! Superego scowled at Id.

I'm just saying. A simple solution would've been to keep your legs shut and say no. Id shrugged.

"Okay…" I leaned my head forward a little, indicating I didn't understand the moral of her story.

"My point is, some people 'peak' in high school. Ever hear of the expression 'high school years are the best years of your life'? Well, for some people that's true. For other people like us, our lives go on to be better than we could've ever imagined." She smiled, wrapping her arms around me.

"Okay. What am I supposed to do in the meantime?" I asked.

"Just let it roll off your shoulders, and trust Mr. Petersen when he says he'll do everything in his power to protect you. He wants you to get through high school. We all do."

I just exhaled slowly. It felt like she was failing to grasp exactly what it was that I was trying to explain to her.

"Listen, babe. If you keep having severe problems, I'll think about transferring you. How does that sound?" She continued rubbing my shoulder.

"Could I be home schooled?" My lit face up with excitement at the prospect.

Mom burst out into laughter. "And who's going to be here to teach you?"

"I don't know. The dog?" I shrugged, a grin crossing my face.

"Oh, Robin!" She playfully pushed me over.

"Seriously, mom. Can we keep him?" My eyes opened wide with hope.

"You know a dog is major responsibility. And who is going to take care of him?" She glared at me sternly.

"I will." I ached to hear words of approval.

"Who is going to pay for his food, his vet visits, and everything else he needs?" She folded her arms across her chest.

"I'll do stuff around the house." I shrugged.

"Are you saying, you'll actually do your chores and keep your room clean and take care of the dog?" Mom's eyes opened wide in disbelief.

"Sure!" I smiled, hoping to elicit a positive response.

"I'll think about it." She replied dryly, rolling her eyes.

I hated that response. It was almost always followed by a no, two or three days later. But I knew if I pressed her, she'd say no right now without any hesitation.

"What about school?" I eagerly changed the subject, hoping to distract her.

"I don't know what to tell you about school. Why don't you wait and see how the assembly goes? High school may not be the best time in your life, but you have to know that Mr. Petersen and I are trying to make it the best we can for you." She smiled at me.

"I know. It's just hard when the other kids won't leave me alone." My shoulders sagged with despair.

"I know sweetie. Just remember. It isn't forever. You have three and a half years left, and then you never have to see any of them ever again if you don't want to. If you can't make it that long, then we will discuss transferring you. Just please try to work with us, and give Mr. Petersen's new ideas a new chance." Mom half smiled at me, trying to entice some enthusiasm from me.

"I'll try. What's for dinner?" I asked, fully returning her smile.

"I'll fix something. Why don't you take the dog outside and meet me in the kitchen?"

"Okay." Taking my leave, I sought solace from my computer.

November 6, 2006 7:04pm

I talked to mom. She wasn't that helpful. She kept saying that for the bullies, high school is the best times of their lives, and my life will get better once I graduate. If I can hold out that long! She also wants me to have faith in Mr. Petersen. I trust him. I just don't trust Mr. Mitchell! He's such an ass! I asked mom if we could keep the dog. She said she'll think about it. That means no. She just needs to think of reasons why no is an okay answer. I hope everything goes well tomorrow.

Chapter 21

I anxiously awaited some kind of an announcement as I sat silently in homeroom. Looking around at the other students, I couldn't help but wonder if any of them had any clue as to the impending assembly. Everyone appeared busy in their own existence, so I turned my attentions to my desk. For the first time in a while, there were no passes on my desk. A half hearted smile crossed my lips, and I heard the attendant go through our names, seeing who cared enough to show up.

When the alarm sounded, I slowly stood up with the rest of my peers as habit dictated us to travel towards our first period class. I took my seat statuesquely, trying to steal glances from my peers' faces. Did any of them know? Were they all clueless as to the upcoming events that were to transpire?

Patience is a virtue. Superego spouted off her wisdom.

Yeah, one my girl doesn't possess. Id cracked.

Don't worry. There will be an assembly soon enough. You have to allow the administration enough time to put the pieces together properly. Superego casually threw out.

And how long is it going to take them before they realize that something needs to seriously change around here?! Id snapped. *You can't honestly expect that they care enough to change things! They're probably sitting in their offices right now, sitting in their nice vibrating chairs, sipping cappuccinos and laughing at our misery!*

Rubbing my temples, I desperately wanted my inner voices to become obsolete. I took out a pencil, trying to distract myself from my thoughts.

"Well, on the bright side, I don't have any detention." I smiled.

Damn right you don't! You didn't do anything wrong! Id nodded.

Yes she did. She cut classes and used her cell phone during school hours. Superego corrected.

Oh, piss off! I am so sick of arguing with you on what the hell happened! If you don't shut your mouth… Anger flashed in Id's eyes.

Laying my head down in my arms, I listened to the silence around me as I faded off into another realm of consciousness. Even as I went through the motions of my various classes, I still hadn't returned.

November 7, 2008 3:12pm

It was so weird! There wasn't an announcement about the assembly. I could've sworn that Mr. Petersen said there was going to be an assembly! I'm so confused! I'm going to talk to mom about it when she gets home. I'm still worried that the other students are going to find out it was my fault (because I'm getting bullied too much), and they're going to hurt me. I just want to be done with high school!!

Chapter 22

"Hey kiddo. How was school?" Mom smiled at me as she entered the living room.

"It was okay. How was work?" I smirked back at her, not looking up from the dog on my lap.

"The same as every day. How was the assembly?" She flopped down on the couch, changing the subject.

"There wasn't one." I looked at her, confused.

"I thought there was supposed to be one." She returned my sentiment.

"I did too." I shrugged.

"Well, maybe Mr. Petersen needed more time to put things in order." Mom shrugged too.

"I guess." I looked down at the dog. He was sprawled out in my lap, laying on his back. His tongue was hanging out the left side of his mouth as his ears flopped back. I started to laugh.

"What's so funny?" Mom asked.

"Bat dog!" I squealed, gently tugging on the ends of his ears. Mom laughed with me.

"Glad to see you're enjoying him." She petted me as I pet the dog.

"Can we keep him?" I blurted out, immediately wishing I'd had a filter on my mouth.

"I told you, I'll think about it." Mom exhaled her frustrations.

"Just wondering." I shrugged, trying to elude her from my emotional desperation.

"Are you ready for the assembly to happen tomorrow?" Mom continued petting me.

"I guess." I shrugged.

"You guess?" Mom slightly pulled on my hair.

"Ahh. Yeah." I wiggled my head, trying to break free.

"What are your thoughts on it?" She tried to gauge my feelings on the subject.

"I'm nervous." The "What if?" monster jumped at the opportunity to play on my fears.

"Why?" Mom shook her head in confusion.

Because I don't want people to know this is my doing. Because I'm tired of being bullied and this is just another excuse for them to push me into a locker again. Because these kids don't care how I feel, and they're never going to care about anyone but themselves... My heart broke as the echoes of my thoughts whispered into my soul.

I shrugged.

"Come on, honey. Talk to me. Why are you nervous?"

"I don't know." I shrugged again.

"Do you think they'll blame you?" Mom ventured a guess into the dark mind of her adolescent daughter.

"Yeah." I concentrated on petting the ball of fur that was keeping me warm.

"But it's not your fault. It's their fault for their awful behavior, and it's about time they were castigated!" Mom hissed. I snapped back in my seat, taking notice of her anger. It wasn't like mom to get angry. She was the closest thing I knew to a saint!

"I know, but they're still going to blame me." My lower lip slid out, threatening to quiver.

"Don't worry, honey. Everything will be okay. I told you last night that we'll wait and see what happens after the assembly. Either way, things will get better. If I have to transfer you to another school, so be it." Mom stood up, kissing me on the forehead. "Now how about you get ready for dinner?"

"Dinner?" I bolted upright, my face erupting into an emotional array of fireworks.

"You're hopeless!" Mom laughed as she walked away. "Just go change and meet me in the car."

I gently slid Shadow over to an empty section of the couch and I ran upstairs.

November 7, 2006 6:27pm

Mom seemed to be a little confused that we didn't have an assembly today. She thinks that maybe Mr. Petersen needed more time to get things organized. I asked her if we could keep Shadow. She said maybe again. Seriously, she means no, but she just needs a reason why no is okay. Well, Mom and I are going to go to dinner. Hope tomorrow goes well! I just want to get this damn assembly done and over with!

Chapter 23

"Robin, have you seen Shadow?" Mom's voice smacked me out of a sound sleep.

I peeled back the covers to reveal him lying in my arms. Upon hearing mom's voice, he woke up and furiously began wagging his tail.

"Awww. Aren't you two so cute?" She smiled. "It's 7am. You'd better get ready for school."

"But I don't want to," I grumbled to myself. I was cozy curled up next to the dog underneath the covers.

Come on dear. You don't want to be late. Superego nodded.

By all means, rush to get to a place where you're not wanted, so you can learn a bunch of shit that you'll never use again in your life. Id sneered.

Stop that! They wouldn't teach her things that are useless! Superego spat.

Oh ok. They want 'well rounded individuals'. That's why they teach everyone the same boring crap. Id rolled her eyes.

They do that so everyone has the same opportunities as each other. Superego furrowed her brows.

Because everyone is the same... Id shook her head.

I slowly sat up in bed, my cohort much more ready to 'carpe diem'.

"I know, buddy. Give me a minute and I'll take you out." My fingers slid down his back, and he eagerly wagged his tail. I didn't even open my eyes fully to coordinate the clothes I threw on. All I could think about was the fact that I had to use the lavatory, and I was willing to bet the dog did as well.

"Come on! You don't want to be late!" Mom called from her room.

"Do you want to take the dog out?" I shot back, irritated to be awake. I loved sleep. No matter how much time went by, I loved to escape the world by sleeping. Night time, day time, it still didn't matter to me.

"What's the matter with you?" Mom scrunched her face up, searching for clues.

"Sorry." I sighed. I didn't know what else to say.

"Talk to me, honey. What's going on?" Mom couldn't find the answers she sought, so she used the only recourse she knew: nagging.

"I just don't want to go to school." I shook my head as I walked towards the bathroom.

"Why not? Did something happen?"

"No."

"Just worried about the assembly?" She ventured a guess.

"Scratch, scratch." Before I could reply, a dry sound made us both jerk our heads to the door at the top of the stairs. The dog was desperately trying to escape.

"Haha! Aww. You're so cute!" I smiled, bending over to scoop him up. "You really want to go out, don't you?"

"Arf, arf!" He darted towards me to give me a kiss.

"Well, go see grandma! Tell her you want to go outside!" I passed the dog to mom, and darted into the bathroom before she could object.

"Thanks!" She hit the door, and I could hear her footsteps head away from me.

"See you downstairs in a bit!" Jumping into the shower, I knew the "What if?" monster had followed me in. The hot water couldn't shake the feeling that today was going to be a bad day...

224

· ·

I curled up in my usual spot against the wall on the bottom row of the bleachers. When there were large groups of people, I preferred my back against the wall. I felt safer this way.

It was 4th period, and the administration had decided to extend lunch (for those who were fortunate to have the first available lunch period). I could see Mr. Petersen and Mr. Mitchell standing with the police over by the podium. They appeared to be chatting amongst themselves in a nonchalant manner. Looking around the room, I could see the students willingly divide themselves into their respective "cliques". There were some loners sporadically disbursed throughout the room, not making any attempts to fit in or hide.

"Good morning." Mr. Mitchell smiled hollowly into the microphone. "I know that this last minute assembly must come as a surprise, and I apologize for interrupting your daily schedule."

"However, it has come to my attention that despite our best efforts to ensure the safety of the student body by enlisting the help of the Fox Grove Police Department, there are renegade students who have managed to continually harass each other."

"This behavior will not be tolerated, and Mr. Petersen would like to announce the following changes to our school's policy. Mr. Petersen?" Mr. Mitchell took a step back, waiving the freeness of the podium over to the superintendent.

"Thank you, Mr. Mitchell." He offered a brief nod to his associate, then turned to address everyone else. "Good morning, everyone. As Mr. Mitchell stated, we are doing our best to keep everyone safe. However, bullying and harassment continues to roam the halls. This behavior is unacceptable, and will cease! It will not be tolerated, under any circumstances!" His voice began to get an angry edge to it, as if he wanted his words to pierce the false senses of security that adolescence offered.

"Starting today, I am issuing two new policies. The first one is a workshop involving all parties. Whenever Mr. Mitchell receives a complaint regarding bullying, all students will report to his office. The bully will not only receive In School Suspension for three days, but will be teased by the person they teased."

Immediately, the whispers roared through the crowd as thousands of teenagers began chattering quietly to each other. Their concern flowed throughout the auditorium, and Mr. Petersen threw his hands in protest.

"Quiet please! Allow me to finish!" He waited a few seconds for the monotone hisses to die down. "Thank you. As I was saying, a friend of mine brought up the point that most bullies aren't concerned with how they make the other students feel. That is not going to be the case anymore! Bullies will learn what it feels like to be ridiculed for asinine things!" A few students giggled as his word choice.

"Also, I have instituted what will be called the 'Red Ribbon Program.' Over two dozen teachers have already signed up, and I hope that every teacher in every school in Fox Grove will have a red ribbon by the end of the school year."

"If you happen to witness anyone being bullied, and you don't want to formally lodge a complaint with Mr. Mitchell, you can go to any teacher who has a red ribbon outside their door and anonymously tip them off to the shenanigans of your fellow peers." Taking a deep breath, Mr. Petersen puffed out his chest, trying to appear larger.

"Because this is an anonymous program, any student caught violating that policy will be expelled! It is expressly prohibited for a bully to lash out at a student who is trying to protect not only themselves, but their fellow students." His voice became more and more impatient and ired as his words continued to trip over themselves. "Are there any questions?"

A girl on the right side of the bleachers raised her hand.

"Yes. The girl in the purple sweater." Mr. Petersen pointed. "Please, stand up and ask your question."

"Can we report things that have already happened, but nobody knows about?" She asked shyly.

"Absolutely! It is my desire to see that every violent act is handled, and every student held accountable. Was there a specific incident you had in mind?" Mr. Petersen smiled.

"No." The girl quickly sat down.

"Any other questions? Yes! You, young man."

A Goth looking kid with short black hair and black clothes that had chains on them at the top row way behind me stood up. "What if we did something to someone because they did something to us?" He didn't shrink into himself like the girl did. He didn't move. He stood there, statuesque, unfazed by what anyone else thought. But, what was that looming just beneath the surface in his eyes?

"Then we will punish the person responsible for initiating the events, but the student who took matters into their own hand will receive a day of ISS. Any other questions?" Nobody else felt brave enough to stand up in front of their peers.

"Now, would Mr. Justin O'Reilly and Ms. Robin Edwards please come down to the podium?" He scanned the crowd.

All the air rushed out of me as surprise uppercut me in the stomach. My nerves shook my whole body, and my heart thumped wildly in protest. It took every fiber in my being to travel 30 feet to Mr. Petersen. I could see Justin sauntering down out of the corner of my eye, his beautiful smile contorted in an evil, vindictive grin.

"Mr. O'Reilly. Did you threaten Ms. Edwards last week?" Mr. Petersen asked.

"Nope." He turned to gaze up at his buddies as Justin snickered under his breath.

"Mr. O'Reilly. I would appreciate the truth. Did you threaten Ms. Edwards last week?" This time, his words revealed he was not in the mood to play around with a 17 year old.

"Um okay. Yeah. Sure." Justin shrugged.

"And what did you say?" Mr. Petersen must've felt like he was pulling teeth out of a rabid dog!

Poor thing. He's trying to set an example, and he has to deal with a difficult teenage boy. Superego pouted.

I say smack the SOB in the back of the head. That'll show him whose boss! Id cackled.

Stop that! *Mr. Petersen is trying to use his brains to show everyone whose in charge*! *If the kids think violence is acceptable, then everyone will be 'smacking' everyone else*! *That's anarchy*! Superego shook her head.

Not really. We just need to make sure my girl can hit hard enough to knock the other person out. That way, they can't hit her back. The side of her cheek pulled up in a wicked smile.

"I told her to watch her ass, because my sister got jumped in prison because that bitch had to blame my sister for tripping into her locker." Justin snickered again as my soul tried to shrink away from the sting of his betrayal.

"Was that really Ms. Edwards' fault?" Mr. Petersen leaned into Justin, staring intently with one eye. I could see Justin start to squirm under the scrutiny.

"Yea. Because she pressed charges, my sister's in jail!" He whined.

"Your sister is in jail because she assaulted Ms. Edwards, and she has to face the consequences of her actions. There are consequences that everyone must face, and it's about damn time you kids learned that!" Mr. Petersen fumed into the microphone. The whole auditorium hushed as his curse word echoed.

"Thank you. As I was saying, your sister assaulted Ms. Edwards, and there are consequences to her actions. You cannot threaten Ms. Edwards because your sister can't handle life in jail. Did you ever stop to think how threatening her again would make her feel?"

"No." Justin spoke a little quieter. Everyone could tell that Mr. Petersen was getting angrier and angrier with every moment that he was not seeing the results he wanted.

"Now, Ms. Edwards. Please tell Mr. O'Reilly how that made you feel." Mr. Petersen extended a hand, slightly pushing me towards my enemy.

"Um, well, it really made me sad. And mad." I mumbled, resisting Mr. Petersen's advancement.

"And why did it make you feel that way?" Mr. Petersen asked.

" Because."

"Because why?"

" Because it's not my fault your sister's in jail. She's in jail because she's a bitch!" I spat at Justin, a smirk forming on my left cheek.

You tell him, girl! Id cheered, throwing a fist in triumph.

That language is awful. Superego frowned.

"My sister's not a bitch!" Justin fumed.

"Oh yeah, okay." I mocked, rolling my eyes. "She hit me every single day! I never did anything to her! It's not my fault someone in jail is giving her a taste of her own medicine!"

"You just can't handle it because you're a whiny bitch!" Justin screamed. The auditorium "oooed" at the sense of trouble.

"At least I'm not someone's bitch in prison!" I shot back. The students roared at my words.

"Enough, you two! Justin, do you understand that Robin has a right not to be assaulted, and that you have no right to threaten her?? Mr. Petersen asked.

"Whatever." Justin rolled his eyes.

"That's not the correct answer, young man. Would you like to try again?" Mr. Petersen stared intently at him.

"Yeah, I guess so." He shrugged.

"Good. Now Mr. Mitchell will escort you down to his office so that you he can assign you two weeks of ISS." Mr. Petersen smiled. My evil nature couldn't help but throw Justin a "ha ha" smile.

"Two weeks?! But I thought you said three days!" Justin whined, protesting his punishment.

"Let me make myself perfectly clear, everyone. The longer it takes a bully to consider the other person's feelings, the longer their detention assignment will be. Am I understood?" The crowd mumbled a variety of positive responses.

"Now, Ms. Edwards. Do you feel better now that Mr. O'Reilly understands how you feel?" Mr. Petersen rubbed my back.

"Kind of." I smiled up at him. Actually, I felt a lot better being given the chance to express myself, as well as stand up for myself.

"Good. You may report to whatever class you normally have scheduled now. Please keep in mind that these new policies will be enforced strictly and thoroughly." Mr. Petersen dismissed everyone.

As I began merging with the herd of other students, I saw my Mom leaning up against the door. Standing up, she headed over to meet me halfway.

"Hey! What are you doing here?" I threw my arms around her neck.

" I just wanted to see how it was going to go. You've been nervous the past couple of days for nothing!" She laughed.

"Yeah, I guess so." I leaned my left ear into my left shoulder.

"Shall we go shopping?" She asked, wrapping her arm around my shoulder.

"I guess. Am I leaving school?" I asked, throwing my arm around her waist.

"Yep! I already told the main office you were coming home with me." We began walking towards the main doors, where mom's car patiently waited for us.

"What are we going shopping for?" I asked.

"Well, I figure we're going to need a leash, and a collar, and some kibble…" Mom started.

"We're keeping the dog?!" I jumped up, causing mom to pause in her tracks.

"Yes, silly. We're keeping the dog." She continued walking.

"Hot damn!" I squealed in delight.

"I'm glad to see you're happy." She said.

"How come we're keeping him?" I asked, puzzled. "I mean, not that I'm complaining, but I didn't think you were that keen on the idea of getting a dog."

"Well, you did offer to do chores and take care of him, right?" Mom asked.

"Absolutely!" I nodded.

"Plus, I can see he makes you happy. I think you would've been a lot more nervous about the assembly if he wasn't around to distract you." Mom climbed into the car. "But, remember. You promised to take good care of him. And you'd better start behaving in school. No more skipping classes."

"Ay, ay, captain!" I saluted.

That was the longest car ride of my life. I couldn't wait to get home and play with my new best friend!!

November 8, 2006 2:31 pm

Today was awesome! Mom totally surprised me! She said we could keep the dog! I'm so happy! The assembly wasn't too bad. I got to tell Justin off in front of everyone, and he got three weeks' detention for not shutting up! Haha! Jackass! Well, I'm going to take Shadow for a walk! I'm so happy! I finally have a friend!

Chapter 24

Time is one of those relative terms that people throw around. Sometimes, they are referring to an appointment that must be kept. Other times, they are using it as a schedule guideline. One thing remains true no matter how you are referring to time. It always marches forward. It may be slower than you'd like, or too fast, but time marches on.

The assembly was several weeks ago, and the halls had become eerily quiet. Even as the Fox Grove Police Department had retrieved all of its officers and left the students alone and unguarded, bullying had gone way down. Everyone was aware that if they were caught bullying, they would be humiliated in front of their peers, and then suspended. It was a fate worse that death. At least, to a teenager it was.

I'd heard through the whispers of the halls that a couple of boys were expelled for picking on a girl who used the "Red Ribbon" program. I guess Mr. Petersen had been serious about kicking students out.

I'd stopped skipping classes. The other students thought it wasn't worth the risk to harass me, and left me alone to stare at the picture of

Shadow that I had taped to the front of each and every school book. I much rather enjoyed the peace and quiet than being harassed every day!

I'd also begun to walk through the halls with my head up. I no longer felt like I was a bad kid, and I no longer felt divided within my soul. I wasn't vengeful, and I wasn't trying to desperately obtain peace. In the end, I had gotten what I wanted. I was being left alone. I wasn't bullied anymore, and I had a friend who cared about me regardless of what happened or what I said or did. So what if he had four legs and a tail?

Today, I was feeling particularly brave as I entered the cafeteria. Did I dare to sit at a table that other students occupied, or would I eat my lunch sitting in the corner like I always did? I scanned the room, hoping to spy any available room at any lunch table. That loner Goth kid was eating lunch by himself. For some reason, nobody else would sit with him.

Come on, honey. Go over and have a seat. Superego smiled.

Yeah. He doesn't look that bad. Besides, he doesn't need the whole table for himself! Id smiled in agreement.

"Is it okay if I have a seat?" I asked, blinking at him.

"Sure. Go ahead." He shrugged.

"Thanks." I slid onto the bench. "My name's Robin. What's yours?"

"Derreck. Call me D." He looked up at me, and that's when I recognized the glint I'd seen at the assembly.

I'd know that look anywhere! It was the look of heartache that came with being ostracized your whole life for being different. It was the pain of rejection that came from years of torment by other kids. Most of all, it was the look of hopelessness. The look that said you thought of yourself as worthless, because that's what everyone else said you were.

"It's nice to meet you, D. Want to see a picture?" I smiled at him.

"Sure." He looked up at me as I dug around in my bag for any one of my school books.

"I just got a dog a couple of months ago. His name is Shadow." I pushed the book towards him.

"He looks like a starving ewok!" D erupted in laughter.

"Nuh uh! Shut up!" I scowled, playfully furrowing my eyebrows.

As the lunch period continued, the pain from rejection that lingered deep within his soul began to fade from the forefront, and I knew that the nightmare of high school was over.

www.ingramcontent.com/pod-product-compliance
Lightning Source LLC
Chambersburg PA
CBHW030409020726
47493CB00003B/991

9 780578 001753